SEP 2 5 2014

BEYOND THE PALE MOTEL

Also by Francesca Lia Block

BEYOND
THE PALE
MOTEL

FRANCESCA LIA BLOCK

St. Martin's Press ⧑ New York

BEYOND THE PALE MOTEL. Copyright © 2014 by Francesca Lia Block. All rights reserved. Printed in the United States of America. For information, address St. Martin's Press, 175 Fifth Avenue, New York, N.Y. 10010.

www.stmartins.com

The Library of Congress Cataloging-in-Publication Data is available upon request.

ISBN 978-1-250-03312-3 (hardcover)
ISBN 978-1-250-03311-6 (e-book)

St. Martin's Press books may be purchased for educational, business, or promotional use. For information on bulk purchase, please contact Macmillan Corporate and Premium Sales Department at 1-800-221-7945, extension 5442, or write specialmarkets@macmillan.com.

First Edition: September 2014

10 9 8 7 6 5 4 3 2 1

For b.c.
and C.Y.

You can talk about all aspects of sex and death in this world, but love still remains a monster that scares people away. I don't know why. Maybe because we all secretly want it so much. Or, at least I do. For me, it's worth the devastation. It's the thing I most desire and I'll continue to seek it out no matter what, no matter how far gone I am. No matter that I am way, way beyond the pale.

#1

At Head Hunter we massaged the scalps of our clients as if they were our lovers; we swept their snipped hair up off the shiny black floor ("A mirror for the Peeping Toms," my best friend, Bree, joked); we sterilized the combs and brushes in blue liquid-poison Barbicide, in glass jars; we basked in the light of pale pink glass chandeliers and blasted nineties music. The Crystal Method, Marilyn Manson, Nirvana, the stuff we loved when we were young and fucked-up, going to raves and grunge shows. Our development had probably been arrested back then, which was why no other music affected us as much. They say addicts tend to get stuck at the age they started using.

Bree and I got sober with the help of the same AA sponsor, Shana, a hot lesbian documentary-film producer, and the black coffee that we drank all day like we used to guzzle Jack. Which was better than shooting

Barbicide; we knew a boy who had killed himself with it and we both got clean the day after his funeral.

Another thing had changed for Bree and me in the last eleven years—the birth of her son, Skylar, whose school picture smiled at me from the corner of my mirror so I could look at him all day long. The green and darker-green-ringed eyes gazed up from under the thatch of brown hair, pouring energy into my arms and wrists when they tired, soothing the ache in my temples when the hairspray fumes got to me at the end of the day.

"Sky-Sky asked me if you could take him to his baseball tryouts in two weeks?" Bree said over the sound of the blow-dryer as I styled her hair.

I sometimes wondered why Skylar wanted me, not his mom, to take him to things like this. Maybe he was less worried about having to impress me. Bree wasn't demanding of Skylar, but she was such a perfectionist herself that he couldn't help but feel some pressure.

"That is, if you're still here after Dash eats you alive," she added.

"I'd come back from the dead to take Skylar to baseball," I told her. "But I hope I get eaten a little at least." My husband, Dash, was arriving home from a gig in San Francisco that night.

"The way you look right now, I don't think it'll be a problem."

My bob was freshly dyed jet-black, my foundation minimal enough to reveal the freckles on my pale skin, but my brown eyes were heavily lined. I wore high-heeled suede boots and a red silk kimono wrap dress printed with pink peonies and white cherry blossoms. Even though the fabric was soft, it made my skin itch; I was most comfortable in dark vintage dresses, or dark denim jeans, but I was trying to get my husband to devour me again. Like when we met. Back then, when he wasn't touching me, he was staring at me with eyes hotter than his hands. Six feet two inches with a shaved head and tatted biceps, he convulsed on the stage at Outer Space. I'd never been with anyone like that. My nipples tingled, I was always wet, a permanent state of arousal. "Please let me have your baby," I would beg, the words orgasming out of my mouth before I could stop them. He would kiss me shut. Over a decade later I was thirty-six and the clock was ticking so loudly it would keep me awake all night while he snored next to me.

I wanted Dash's baby, I told myself, because of how much I loved Dash. Now I wonder if maybe I just wanted to hold on to him. And to make a child who would never leave me.

But I had left my own mother, ultimately, trying to get back at her for abandoning me so many times. At least I had Dash and Skylar and Bree. No matter what, I had them.

"So hot, Catt," Bree promised, checking out my push-up-bra-enhanced cleavage in the mirror. Not me, but Bree is hot. Always. I had dyed her hair pale pink this time. Most people over the age of nineteen couldn't easily get away with pink hair unless they were rock stars, but Bree could, even at our age. And a bit of a rock star she was, at least at Head Hunter. She had on a white lace dress and pink slip she had designed and made, along with over-the-knee platform boots of black Spanish leather, her pale eyes always slightly askew as if she were looking through the air at something better than you will ever see.

"Thanks, baby blue. I tried to channel you today."

She turned her head, reached up, and kissed me on the lips, hers like a MAC ad. Ample Pink gloss that costs $20 for a tiny tube. I bought some once but put it in the back pocket of my jeans and it slid out and into the toilet bowl. I will never be Bree. Sometimes her full-frontal kisses made me have to squeeze my thighs together even though I could never sleep with her again—not sober; I'd compare our bodies the whole time and it would ruin the experience. (She is tall and lithe, while I was shorter and curvy. "Voluptuous," Bree said, but that wasn't always the word I thought of when I saw my reflection.) More important, Bree was family and I didn't want to risk losing her if something went wrong. She had pretty much expressed the same sentiment after the third time she and I slept together, in a threesome with Baby Daddy, and she conceived Skylar.

The first time Bree and I slept together was the night we met—just teenagers at a party in the Hollywood Hills. I don't know how I got there. But I remember that it was the Fourth of July because you could see the

Hollywood Bowl fireworks from the balcony, and I remember every detail about Bree. She was wearing a white satin 1920s nightgown with a big silver zipper inserted down the front and combat boots. Half of her head was shaved. Nine Inch Nails was playing and she was singing along.

I went up to her and said, "We're going to be friends forever."

She said, "How do you know?"

I said, "I just do." Then I said, "I like your hair." I told her I wanted to be a stylist because you could make people feel good every day.

"And make ourselves feel good by partying every night," Bree added.

We went out on the balcony under the fireworks and snorted some coke and drank some more. I marveled at her firework-illuminated beauty even in that high and drunken state. Somehow we were in bed together. She smelled like white roses and felt as satiny and fragile as her dress. A man Bree knew—a fairly well-known actor from a TV show—came into the room and got under the covers with us but I mostly ignored him. He touched her breasts and my ass and jerked off while we kissed and put our fingers inside each other, as if we were petting the shyest animals, until we fell asleep. She woke later, feeling sick, and I walked her to the bathroom and held her forehead and her tiny, heaving torso while we knelt on the black-and-white tile floor. Afterward I wiped her face with a wet washcloth and found a clean pack of toothbrushes in a drawer for her to use.

In the morning I saw that the room we'd slept in had dark wood furniture and very white curtains and sheets. The sun shone through cathedral-style windows, making my hangover worse, and in the distance I could see the palm-treed hills hazed with smog. Bree and the man and some other people and I went out to breakfast. We ate pancakes—Bree's stomach was better by then—and wore our sunglasses and smoked cigarettes on the patio. Bree had a black Mercedes SUV that her parents had bought her when she turned sixteen and she blasted the music so loud it rumbled in my chest.

"You're right," she said, when she dropped me off at my house later that afternoon.

"About what?"

"We're going to love each other forever."

It hadn't been forever yet, but it had been eighteen years.

"What did you do this weekend?" I asked grown-up, sober Bree, spritzing the last bit of hairspray on her bubble-gum-colored locks.

"Baby Daddy had Skylar so I went on another FU Cupid date."

I scowled at her in the mirror.

"I know. I have no idea why I go."

Bree told me she kept her profile up for the hell of it, an ego boost after pandering to female egos all day.

That part I understood, although one of the female egos I pandered to was hers. I loved her enough to keep doing it no matter what, and it had gotten easier after I met Dash.

"This guy was fine, though," she said. "A dermatologist, if you can believe it. Black Irish. Free Botox." I didn't think she needed to get the botulinum toxin injected into her muscles to freeze them, but she said it was preventative. "And he wrote to me like one hundred and fifty times before I responded."

Honestly, in spite of the fact that I knew a few people who had gotten married to someone they'd met on the Internet, I wasn't sure how safe it was. But Bree said that was part of the thrill and that she could take care of herself. At least she never invited them over when Skylar was around.

"Which monster?" I asked, though I could already guess.

She shrugged and eyed her reflection. "A bit of a Vampire."

Since we were in our twenties, Bree and I had come up with names for all the guys we met. Vampires were elegant, refined, and sensual. Dash was a Zombie, which sounded like a bad thing but was actually hot according to our system. Zombies were big and brawny, a little clumsy, but ravenous sexually. They wanted to come back to life and you could give them that, which was empowering. Goblins were the businessmen we never dated. Ghouls were trouble—junkies and alcoholics, the ones that trickled in and out of my meetings but couldn't stay sober. Manticores, with their three rows of proverbial teeth, could look like anything but would devour you whole. Woman-eaters. We had taken to writing about all of them in our blog, *Love Monster,* in which we collected the things in life that made it tolerable after alcohol had been removed from the equation. Although I had become the main contributor, the idea for *Love Monster* had been Bree's. She thought it was important to keep track of our distractions and fascinations.

"What did you do?" I asked Bree. With Dr. Vampire.

"*Aloo gobi* at Lotus Eater, and then we went to Sound to see some Swedish band. My ears are still ringing. I'm too old for this. What's up with that sound system?"

"He's really a dermatologist?"

"Yes. But he should do porn. Serious. His dick is like James Deen's."

She stopped as the door jingled open and our first customer came in, Stu, a TV producer who lived in the Valley but slummed in Silver Lake to have his cut buzzed weekly by Bree, probably just so he could stare at her in the mirror. So I didn't get to find out more about the Vampire's penis. I didn't mind; I was thinking about resurrecting Dash. How he would rip off the itchy red dress and pump me full of life. *Maybe I can get him to lose the condom tonight,* I thought.

"Check that out," Stu said, nodding at the TV and flexing his hands as Bree tied the black nylon apron around his thick neck.

The sound was off but a selfie of a pretty young woman smiled from the screen. Under the image were the words HOLLYWOOD SERIAL KILLER STRIKES AGAIN?

Stu hit the volume button on the remote and scrutinized the TV. His eyes were such a pale color the pupils looked like spots of black ink. He rubbed his fingers over his slightly receding chin. "They found this one in the hills like the first. Her name's Adrienne something. Banks, I think. Model/actress, same as before. He cut off this one's legs. Brutal shit."

The girl before, Mandy Merrill, was found by hikers, not far from the Hollywood sign. Her arms had been cut off, severed precisely at the shoulder joints.

Bree and I looked at each other. There were instant tears in both our eyes. She took the remote from Stu and shut off the TV.

"Arms, legs. It's like he's collecting," said Stu. "I wonder if someone is going to rip it off for a series or something. I might have to get on that. Oh, snap, did I just say *rip it off*? Bad pun, Stu, bad."

Bree and I exchanged another glance; we played monster dating games, but neither of us had much tolerance for the real thing.

When I was a teenager, they caught Jeffrey Dahmer and I was haunted by his pale, bloated face—the petulant lips and dead blue predator eyes. How he had lured all those young men, killed them, violated their corpses, cut them into pieces which he stored in his refrigerator. Sometimes he consumed parts of the bodies.

I'd read somewhere that he wanted a dead lover because that was the perfect kind—they didn't move or speak. He'd even tried drilling into some of their skulls while they were still alive and injecting acid into their brains to animate them. Looking back on it, I wondered if the metaphor of dismemberment, brutality, and monster-making reflected my own confused and agonized teenage state of mind. I thought I'd transcended all that as an adult, a sober, married woman, but with the mention of the Hollywood Serial Killer the obsessive fear came back like a needle to my spine.

"Okay, that's enough," Bree said, frowning at Stu.

I rode a surge of nausea and tried to pretend it was because I was pregnant. *Maybe I will be after tonight,* I thought. Better to think of that than of what was happening to these lovely, severed girls who had only ever wanted, I was sure, like me, to be loved by someone.

Looking at Skylar's photo again, I could almost smell his floppy hair—baseball-field dust and chamomile-honey baby shampoo. Skylar made everything feel better, but my heart still ached, overfull with love and fear.

After work I decided to go to Body Farm even though I'd have to redo my hair and makeup, change back into the dress and the boots that crunched, like teeth, the bones of my feet. I needed to sweat off the news and Stu's response to it.

The gym was a small, mirrored mini-mall world full of eastside hipsters, not unlike the place I worked all day, except here they dealt in muscles instead of hair. Big Bob, the owner, was training a ridiculously gorgeous young woman I hadn't seen before. She looked like a pageant contestant—high ponytail, enormous breasts, tiny waist, Bambi eyes and legs—white-hot beautiful even by Body Farm standards, which was saying a lot.

"Cute dress," she said to me. Genuinely sweet. I said thank you, secretly glad Dash wasn't there to see her.

Bob was kneeling over with his hand on her thigh, stretching it back toward her head, fondling the muscle, and as I passed, he turned and looked at me in a way that sent an air-conditioned blast down my dress. His arm was much thicker around than her leg, and his skin gleamed with spray tan and oil. I've never liked Bob, and between his energy and the plethora of hot, young girls whom I tended to compare myself to, I always thought I'd stop going to Body Farm. Creepy name anyway, isn't it? But I stayed because Scott was there. And, if I'm honest, because it had a reputation for "making" the best bodies in town, or at least Big Bob was known for that. I didn't train with him though; he charged $200 an hour and scared the crap out of me.

"How's my girl Bree?" Bob asked, flashing some teeth.

I said fine and walked away.

Scott was there that night, as always, standing with his hands in the pockets of his nylon Nike sweatpants.

He never wore shorts because he'd had some surgery on his leg in his early twenties, although I was never quite sure exactly what it was for, just that he had a big scar he didn't like anyone to see, that he smoked medical marijuana to help deal with some residual pain, and that he couldn't do high-impact exercise.

Sometimes I wondered if Scott ever left Body Farm. We used to tease him about sleeping on the machines and showering in the bathroom before we got there.

He didn't fit any of the monster categories. Which is why we loved him. And had never dated him. Sometimes it takes a monster to scare away the stress of daily life.

Smelling of expensive, subtle cologne, Scott gave me a kiss on the cheek. "Hey, Catt."

"Hi, sweet one."

He asked how I was.

"Ugh. Freaked-out. Did you hear about that other girl who was killed?"

Scott shook his head. "It's horrifying. Makes you want to go far away and never come back."

Rick and Todd, with their matching buzz cuts, Aztec tattoos, and Air Force 1s came over, oblivious of what we had been discussing. "Good timing, Catt. We were just telling Scotty here his hair is getting a little long, don't you think?" Rick said.

Toddrick, as we called them, liked to tease Scott about being vain, even more meticulous than they were. His hair was always perfectly cut, by me, of course. He never let anything about him get messy.

I touched his neat, well-shaped head. "Looks good to me," I said. "Now you, on the other hand . . ."

Rick backed away. "No way, Edwina Scissorhands, I won't go anywhere named for cannibals."

"Yeah, Blow is much better for a hair salon." That was the place in Boys Town where Toddrick went for their matching cuts.

"I'd rather do blow than have my head hunted."

"I'd rather *be* blown," Todd offered.

"Okay, cats and dogs, let's not get crazy here," Scott said. "Besides the horrors on the news, how's it going?" he asked me, pointing at Todd to get on the lat machine.

"Dash is back tonight."

Scott raised his eyebrows. "You sure you want to get sweaty now? Won't there be enough of that later this evening?"

"Not the way things have been going unless I play it right. But I gotta work off the jitters."

I'd been nervous about trying to get my husband's attention; now I was thinking about dead girls. As I picked up the first set of weights and smelled the tang of metal, I thought of the girl whose arms had been sawed off, the other without legs. In that moment I was grateful for my own body, which beat with life, especially in Dash's embrace.

"Well, just don't forget how lucky that man is to have you," Scott said, trying to make me feel better, the way he always did.

Dash, that "lucky man," and I moved into the bungalow when we got married. He actually carried me over the threshold on our wedding night, into the empty rooms—just the bed and the vanilla gardenia candles and bouquets of pink and white peonies Bree had installed secretly that morning. Dash knew how to fuck; he was big, and hard, and the best I'd ever had, and knowing that he was my husband had made me wetter and more responsive than ever.

"I think you just set a record, babe," he said, when I came again.

Our place was built onto the side of a hill, overlooking the lake, the palm trees and cypress, bougainvillea and oleanders. You have to climb up a steep, white staircase, pass through the thick arches into the courtyard with its ferns, bamboo, and koi pond. Inside, one bed, one bath. No space for a kid, Dash said, but I knew the tiny office where my desk and futon were could be converted if necessary. Wood floors, white built-ins, including a mirror over the fireplace. The fireplace is not safe to use, but Dash lit a fire in it anyway sometimes. Pink-and-black tile in the kitchen and bathroom. Probably lead-based because of how it shines but I didn't mind. I had once done a whole *Love Monster* post on the toxic beauty of 1950s bathroom tile.

Our poisoned bungalow was all I ever wanted, really. When Dash was there, anyway. He's as big as the Cal King mattress and didn't even fit in the claw-foot tub. His giant black Docs sat by the front door because we agreed we wanted the floor pristine. We had meditated together every morning and before bed, slipping the cool, clicking beads of the malas between our fingers. My mala's made of rhodochrosite, pink and marbled, and his is wood. As a teenager I'd used a rosary to help me fall asleep at night, especially during that Dahmer phase, when I couldn't stop thinking about heads in refrigerators and organs in Ziploc bags. After I got sober and met Dash, Catholicism started making less sense than Eastern religions.

It was better than drinking, better than cigarettes and caffeine, our meditation practice, our lovemaking, our life. But it had been changing in the last year, a slow decline. I didn't want to admit it to myself.

As I headed into the bungalow, our neighbor from down the block ran by in a streak of neon short-shorts and tan skin. Dash and I called her Skipper; she was always running, sprinting, skipping backward, sometimes twice a day, nose, breasts, and butt pert, high ponytail bobbing. Must have been one of those model/actresses that come to this city in droves, I'd thought. Not quite pretty enough to be Barbie; more like her sidekick.

I'd almost asked her to dinner once but decided that between Dash's gigs, our AA meetings, Head Hunter, and Body Farm, my husband and I had enough estrogen in our lives.

That night I was making him *pho* with fresh herbs, rice noodles, shrimp. For dessert—freshly baked chocolate chip cookies, which were our favorite. The smell of butter, sugar, and chocolate, and lemongrass, ginger, and jasmine tea, filled the kitchen. When I heard Dash at the door, my heart flipped like a fish about to be reeled in. I wished I hadn't worn the red dress all day. I should have just put it on after work, but I'd wanted to pump myself up, see if any men looked twice to remind me I was worthy of Dash.

I called out, "Hi, baby," waited, counted to ten, trying not to rush to him.

He came in while I was crushing the garlic, popping the skin with the flat of a knife, and I glanced up and saw that his face looked different, white and still. Black T-shirt and black jeans as always. Muscles defined by pale blue veins. I always felt small around him, which was part of what turned me on. I was really heavy in high school, and even though I'd lost a lot of weight after getting sober, I was still a big girl. But not in his arms.

"Hey, baby, you okay?" I put down the garlic, wiped my hands on my fruit-patterned, vintage apron, and went to him, untying the apron strings to show off my dress.

He kissed me, but it was in a distracted way, eyes

open. He was chewing peppermint gum but I could taste the tobacco and caffeine on his lips.

"What's wrong, baby?"

"I'm just tired. Smells good in here." He moved away a little too quickly, and something fell and shattered inside of me, like when I had dropped my favorite gold shot glass that time. I should have known. Women's intuition and all. But who wants to know? Delusion is so much more pleasant in the end.

When he finally told me, it was dawn and we were lying awake, sweating, not touching each other. My cat, Sasha, had abandoned her usual post on my pillow. The fan wasn't cooling the room, just making an annoying sound as it blew hot air around. I wanted an icy-cold gin and tonic more than anything at that moment so I went through the acronym of AA warning signs, HALT: Hungry, Angry, Lonely, Tired. I wasn't hungry. I was tired for sure and very lonely, even with Dash lying there beside me in his underwear. I was angry.

"What?" I said finally. The word that always preceded our arguments.

"What what?" He groaned and turned away from me, onto his side. His back looked meaty and pale in the light that was starting to finger us through the blinds.

"Something's wrong," I said.

Dash sat up with an exhale and rubbed his forehead. "You always think something is wrong."

"Well, is it? You haven't touched me, you hardly ate."

"So this signifies a problem? Because I didn't fuck you after being up for, like, twenty-four hours? Because I wasn't in the mood for *pho*? Seriously, Catt?"

"Just tell me," I said. I was quietly leaving my body already at that point, everything going numb as I slid out of my skin and observed myself from some odd spot on the ceiling. I looked bloated and washed-out and my hair was tangled. *Get up,* I told myself. *Leave now. Don't listen to him say it.* But I couldn't move.

"Okay, fine. You can't just let anything lie, can you."

I don't want you to lie anymore, I thought. In that moment, even before he said it, everything I had been denying was becoming clear.

"There's someone," Dash said.

"What do you mean there's someone?" I just couldn't move any part of my body. He had met someone? On his trip he'd met someone he liked, that was all. He hadn't actually . . .

"There's been someone. It's serious."

I doubled over, grabbing my stomach, feeling the layer of fat there. He'd socked me in the gut with two words and I couldn't breathe.

"What are you talking about?" I whispered. But my voice was getting louder and louder. "Who did you meet?"

He wouldn't look at me.

The thoughts careened into each other as they fought

to get out of my mouth. "Who is she? How long has it been? And you're telling me now? Tonight?"

"You asked me *what*. You always want to know. What, what, what? Okay, I told you. Are you happy?"

The ice pain in my abdomen flared to heat that spread through my whole body. My heart was pounding like I was on the Body Farm treadmill. "What the fuck? Am I what? Happy? Get the fuck out of here, Dash."

He got up and put on his jeans. The belt, decorated with skulls, was still threaded through the belt loops, and the heavy metal buckle clanked.

He pulled on his T-shirt without looking at me. His back was huge, straining the cotton fabric as if it might tear. I realized I would never touch him again. Everything irrevocably over. One of us might as well have been killed in that instant. And it was probably me. My first death of nine. Who was the zombie now?

When I was in my early twenties, I had a dog I'd found on the street. A gentle beagle-and-pit-bull mix I called Pinkie. I walked and fed her, she slept on my bed. It was good for me, at that time, to have something to take care of, even though I couldn't care for myself. Then the seizures began. Her body hurtling against the walls, mouth lathering, shit everywhere. Afterward she wouldn't recognize me, would just growl for a long time. Once, after an episode, she looked at me without recognition. When I reached for her, she bit my hand, breaking the skin, though it wasn't that deep. The meds they gave me for her didn't work, the tumor they discovered was inoperable, and finally I decided to put her down. I was drunk. It was raining. I drove her to the vet, who told me I should leave, that it wouldn't be pleasant to watch. She was still big and strong, nothing seemed wrong to look at her. The vet walked into the back room and she followed him, trotting along, trusting. Sometimes I still dreamed of her bony head, her lopsided eyes, and long, graceful legs.

"I'm sorry," Dash said. For the first time since I'd asked the final *what*, his voice sounded human, even kind. This made it worse. I wanted to grab him, tear him back from wherever he was. I was going to be alone. I was going to die alone like my mother. Unless I could get him to stay.

"Wait, please. Dash. Talk to me."

He shook his head.

"Why?" I screamed. "What did I do? What happened?"

"It's not about you and me," he said and his voice was cold again. "It's about me. And her."

#2

I didn't find out who "her" was for a while. If I hadn't been so scared to know, I would have tried harder. I didn't want it to be real. Dash had been the center of my existence for almost as long as I'd been sober. What would happen to me if I fully acknowledged that he was gone, that he had fallen in love with someone else? That I would never have his child, or maybe anyone's child? Would I drink again? Would I perish without my husband's love to save me?

In 2002 Bree and I were newly sober and Dash spoke at a meeting. When he was up there speaking, no one could look away. His smile was a sexy grimace and his tattoos mesmerized, like a maze your eyes wanted to follow to their center. Lotus flowers and poetry in Latin curved over his biceps, Aztec symbols inked his neck, a snake slithered up his calf and disappeared inside the leg of his shorts. He told about the first drink at twelve, the first hard drugs at thirteen. Foster homes and fights and beatings. Whole periods of time forgotten. It made my childhood look pretty good in comparison. "It gets better," he said. "It really does." That was what I needed to hear.

Bree insisted on taking me to see his band play at Sound the next weekend. She could tell I was smitten; he was all I had talked about that week. We were both scared of going to a bar so early in our sobriety, and Bree was pregnant, but we vowed to keep an eye on each other the whole night. We parked under the stone bridge and walked along the deserted street, up the dirty stairs, across the littered pass to the club. I smelled alcohol in the air right away, but by the end of the night it wasn't Jack I wanted.

When Dash came onstage, I clung to Bree's firm, little biceps to steady myself. We were too near the speakers. My ears rang and rang; there'd be pain in the morning. I guzzled my cranberry and soda, staring at the way this man bared his teeth.

"She had a neck like a swan but her tits were fake. There was a dead body in the Sliver Lake. I said, 'Baby, baby, I'll keep you safe.' She said, 'Wipe that smile offa your face.'"

I guess it had something to do with an illusion of safety. As if no one would mess with me if I were his. In middle school I'd been bullied by the mean boys more than the girls, who pretty much ignored me. I was like a magnet for the boys' comments. "Fat ass." "Zit face." Sometimes I wondered if the hypersexuality

I tried to hide from the world was showing through, so awkward and ashamed of itself that it drew taunts. I touched myself to fall asleep every night and daydreamed about sex in the light. Or maybe it was that those mean boys smelled my fear like dogs do. I hung my head when I walked past them, wondering if they knew my secrets.

When I lost some weight and my skin cleared up, when I learned how to do my hair and makeup, and dress to flatter my cleavage and calf muscles, I still half expected a surprise attack at every turn. The drinking helped. But now it was gone. Now I needed a mean boy in the body of a 250-pound man more than ever.

But of course mean boys are just that.

Once a week we went out for Thai food at one of the late-night places on Santa Monica Boulevard or shopped at the Hollywood farmers market and I made him dinner. Then we had great, famished sex. I wondered why we didn't see each other more, but he told me he had to rehearse a lot so I left it at that. After a few months we came home for dinner and he was tugging at the button of my blouse when I stopped him.

"I'd really like to see you more often." I had been working up to this for weeks, with Bree's coaching. "I feel like it's hard to get to know someone just once a week."

He dropped to the couch, kneading his fingers, squinting up at me. Sasha sat watching us from behind the door with her psychic green eyes. She still didn't trust Dash.

"It's not like I'm seeing anyone else," he said. "I rehearse a lot. And I go to meetings."

"Maybe we could go to one together sometime," I ventured. My body had already attached to him and didn't want to let go so soon. I knew that I'd back down and continue to see him on his terms if I had to.

"I go to SLAA. You know what that is?"

"Sex and Love Addicts?"

He nodded. Sasha sat there, still watching. "Yeah. I've been going for six months. It really helps."

"Like, what?" I asked, my heart pounding through my thin shirt. "Porn or prostitutes or . . ."

"I haven't been active in six months," he said. "I think it's better if we don't talk about it too much."

I looked down at my hands, wishing I'd gotten a manicure. The black polish was chipped, the skin was dry.

"Okay," I said.

"Are you okay?"

I didn't know.

"Maybe I should go?"

"Yeah."

That night I cried when he left, imagining that even if we got through this, he would cheat on me with groupies or, at the very least, fantasize about porn stars when we fucked.

The problem was that I couldn't stop thinking about him. I began to imagine him with other women—girls with giant breasts, tiny waists, tan, shaven skin, shiny hair reaching to asses that could almost fit in his hand.

These thoughts made me come hard, but I always dissolved into tears with the last clenchings, humiliated by my own mind.

A few weeks later he called me, we went out for dinner, he said, "You're the one I want to see now, babe." It didn't take much.

While he was inside me, I saw him in my mind with a goddess girl covered in tattoos. Dense, richly colored peonies and butterflies on her arms, a tiger's face on her ass, the cleft of its mouth inked along her crack. In my mind I sat chained to a chair, naked, legs spread. I was watching them, unable to touch myself.

I think we finally got married because he needed someone to care for him and I needed someone to feed, which was its own kind of hunger.

Two weeks had passed since Dash had left with only a small bag of his things. The drapes in the bungalow caught on fire and continued to burn steadily. Daggers shot out of the showerhead. Spiders nested in my hair and formed a web over my mouth and eyes. Sasha lay on my stomach, batting at the web, trying to make things better. On the TV, toddlers seemed to be continually falling out of the sky, caught, if they were lucky, in the arms of strangers who happened to be passing by. Pomegranate seeds were infecting people with hepatitis. In a crime drama a serial killer with dashing cheekbones prepared gourmet meals with human meat. I wondered if the

Hollywood Serial Killer looked like a Hollywood actor; how else had he been able to lure Mandy Merrill and Adrienne Banks? My mala sat by the bed untouched, even though it would probably have helped me to meditate; Dash had taken his beads with him. The only thing that got me out of the house was Bree, who told me I had to use work to get my mind off Dash, and Scott, who told me I had to sweat for the same reason.

Being at both Head Hunter and Body Farm was awful though. Since Dash had left, men that made me uncomfortable before now made my skin slither, and Big Bob, with his vapid eyes and too-bleached teeth, and Stu, salivating like a necrophiliac over pretty murder victims on TV, made my skin want to crawl off my bones.

My husband had left me feeling dismembered, but Mandy Merrill and Adrienne Banks actually had been.

"They were both so hot," Stu said at Head Hunter, while he pawed through a gossip magazine featuring the Hollywood Serial Killings.

"Can you stop talking about those murders, Stu," said Bree as she buzzed his head. "We don't need to hear it."

"So many women come here to get famous, and they have a better chance of doing it by getting killed and chopped into pieces."

Bree and I exchanged a glance in the mirror above his head.

Shut the fuck up, Stu.

If he wasn't Bree's most regular client, I was pretty

sure she'd have thrown him out right then. I was ready to do it myself if he said another word.

The only thing that really got my mind off things was Skylar.

The first time Bree brought him into Head Hunter after Dash left, Sky hugged me for a longer time than usual. "You're going to take me to baseball tryouts next Saturday, right?"

"Of course. It's on the calendar. There's nothing I'd rather do."

"And what about Honey's birthday party this Sunday?"

I looked at Bree, who nodded. "Of course," I said.

Sky's birthday parties had been train-themed since he was two, with the train growing in size, along with him, each year. At the first party he spent the whole time squatting on the floor over his wooden train set with his friend Honey. To get to the other side of the track he'd remain in a squat and hop like a frog. By the time the birthday cake, shaped like a train, of course, was served, he had fallen asleep, and I took a photograph of him lying on his back with his arms flung out, the cake on the bed beside him. When he was three, we hired a guy in a conductor's uniform to bring a kid-size track and train in which Skylar and Honey rode around and around, wearing blue-and-white-striped conductor's hats, with placid expressions on their faces, until he fell asleep again. His fourth and fifth birthdays included more children and took place at the outdoor train museum in Griffith Park. This time the train ride was big enough to hold the grown-ups, too, and after we'd ridden on that, we explored the real trains in the yard. They seemed mildly, hollowly haunted, metal walls echoing with the laughter of children. Sky did not fall asleep on either of these occasions. On his sixth birthday Bree and I took Skylar and Honey on the metro downtown to Olvera Street. After that Skylar outgrew his obsession with trains, which was a good thing, since I didn't know if there was any place where we could easily find a bigger one.

I was taking Sky to Honey's eleventh birthday in Griffith Park but no trains were involved; her mom, Joy, was having a picnic on a hillside. On our way up the hill bikers on their way to a Harley convention zoomed past my car—guys with women on the back, flesh exposed where their shirts rode up, their arms around the dudes, many of whom were built like Dash. There was something so intimate about riding on a motorcycle, holding on with that humming between your legs.

I turned my attention back to Skylar. "When's the last time you saw Honey?"

"My birthday last year," he said. "But we're still on Instagram."

At one point a few months earlier I'd seen Skylar smiling shyly at his iPod Touch and I'd asked what he was doing.

"Messaging Honey."

"What's that smile about?"

He blushed. "We're sort of boyfriend-girlfriend."

"What does that mean?"

"It's complicated."

I'd been concerned until I learned that "it's compli-cated" meant she had informed him of this new status via Instagram on his iPod—he hadn't actually had much to do with the decision—and that being "sort of boyfriend-girlfriend" consisted of saying you were "go-ing out" and messaging each other all day and at least once before bed.

A few weeks later I asked if she was still his girl-friend and he said, "No. She dumped me."

"Are you okay?"

"I'm too young for a relationship anyway." He had that peaceful Buddha baby look on his face and I found my-self wishing I could be more like that about Dash leaving.

After Honey had blocked Skylar for one day on Ins-tagram, they were back to following each other and "still friends."

The Sunday of Honey's eleventh birthday I was feel-ing relieved to be with Sky, finally, for a whole day, but I didn't look forward to having to answer the adults' questions about me. As Sky ran off to join the kids, Honey's mom, Joy, danced up to me, wearing a long Indian gauze skirt and lots of bangles, her hair wafting around her, her baby, Boston, in a sling. Of course she had to ask about Dash. I just shook my head.

"Oh, I'm so sorry," Joy said. "I thought I heard something about that."

I took a plate of crudités and macaroni salad and sat in the shade. A young woman came over to nurse her baby. Great. She pulled out her large, pale breast and smiled dreamily at me while the child suckled. Its eyelids reminded me of a baby bird's.

"How old?" I asked to be polite.

"Six months. His dad is finally able to look at something besides us for three seconds." She nodded beamily over at the dad, who was heaping his plate with food.

Shit. I recognized him. It was Jimmy.

Right before he left us, my dad introduced me to his friend's son, a tall, skinny guitar player. Jimmy came over to the house for dinner, and when he looked at me with his green eyes under twitchy, thick, black brows, as if he saw a pretty young woman and not a fat girl, I knew I'd lose my virginity to him. At the time I didn't question the fact that that my father had introduced us, maybe with this same thought at least vaguely in mind, and that I was sixteen and Jimmy was twenty-one.

For months we went out on hikes in the Hollywood Hills and ate picnics he packed for us. Between the exercise and the turkey sandwiches I lost a bit of weight, but I still felt self-conscious about my size. Jimmy never took me to a restaurant or one of his gigs, the latter, he said, because I was too young to get in. I never questioned the former but hoped it had to do with his being short on funds, a starving artist, rather than that he was ashamed of me. He did give me CDs of his band, a keyboard-heavy goth deal that I thought was pretty sexy sounding. I was into goth myself at the time, which I thought was why my dad had introduced me to Jimmy, although later I realized it all had much more to do with my father's planning his exit from my life. I used to tell myself it was at least an expression of his concern, afraid I would be alone in the world without any male protection.

Once when we were watching a news report about Jeffrey Dahmer, I told my dad that I was scared someone would break in when he wasn't home. We were sitting on the couch and I'd been observing his strong profile, his thick, black hair; I resembled him but had always wanted to look more like my Swedish mother.

Without glancing away from the TV he'd said, "That's why boyfriends are a good idea."

And I wondered why I had grown up to be dependent on men?

Jimmy and I would make out during our hikes or in his Mustang (he still lived with his parents so he couldn't take me home), but he never pressured me to have sex with him and hadn't even seen me completely naked, which I was grateful for. He often referred to my virginity in a romanticized way, and I thought he really liked the idea of waiting until I was eighteen, in spite of any frustration it might cause him. He told me that the longing was feeding his songwriting, and he played me acoustic versions of songs about insecure, voluptuous young girls in chastity belts. I thought this meant he was in love.

Once on the way back from a hike he told me he wanted to stop at this party. I was in jeans and hiking boots, covered with dust, and feeling especially heavy, but he said, "I want you to be part of my life," so I agreed to go.

The party was just under the HOLLYWOOD sign, where we had been hiking that day. *Where the armless body of Mandy Merrill was found.* A ficus tree guarded a brick house full of musicians and groupies. Jimmy introduced me as his friend and wandered off to talk to people, leaving me standing alone in my hiking boots, holding a chilled beer that was warmer than my hands. I remember the seams of my jeans digging into my flesh. Finally I asked Jimmy if we could leave. He gave me a hit of the joint he was holding, put me in the car, and told me he had to go "take a leak." After a long time I went back in and found him exchanging phone numbers with a skinny, blond girl in a slip and stilettos.

"This is my friend Catherine," he told her.

I smiled frozenly and followed him back to the car. There was a full and mocking moon above the ficus tree and the joint was starting to kick in.

"Friend?" I said finally.

"Do you want to be more than friends?" He pulled a

condom and a glass vial from the glove compartment. Mutely, I let him fuck me in the Mustang. Jimmy sniffed the popper and bellowed when he came, but to me the sex felt like nothing—I guess I had left my body—and we broke up the next day. As if without my virginity there was no other bond between us. By then my dad was already long, long gone.

"Catherine? Hi." Jimmy looked as if he was going to kiss my cheek, but then thought better of it. He'd gained some weight and cut his hair. "I almost didn't recognize you. You look good. Have you met my wife, Sara, and our baby, Eli?"

"Yes, hi." Her handshake was weak, but then again she was nursing, so maybe that was taking all her energy. "I actually go by Catt now."

"How do you know Joy and Jake?"

"Honey's best friends with my godson, Skylar."

"And Eli's best friends with Boston," Sara said. I wondered how infants could be best friends but she answered for me. "They get together for nursing dates and bring me and Joy along to provide the refreshments."

Clever girl. The day was too hot, I was sweating, and maybe the macaroni salad had been out too long. Or maybe it was the conversation that was making me queasy. Refreshments?

Jimmy was teaching music lessons and still playing in

local bands. He couldn't be happier to be a dad. Being a
dad was not an easy thing. It was the hardest and best
thing he'd ever done. Sara was amazing. She'd taught
him so much. She was an old soul, even though she was
in her early twenties. They'd met when she signed up for
guitar lessons. How was I? He'd heard I'd gotten married. A musician? Did we have any kids?

That's when I managed to end the conversation and
get away. Skylar and Honey were playing catch, wearing their Dodger regalia. Her arm was almost as good
as his. Still wore her fine, straight hair the way her
mother had styled it when she was a baby, tied with a
ponytail holder so it stuck straight up on her head. I
wondered if Honey and Skylar would be friends always,
if they might even fall in love, get married, and have
children.

I thought of Sara and Joy nursing Eli and Boston, sitting together in a park somewhere, under a jacaranda
tree. Later they might take a Mommy and Me yoga
class (although the *me* part wasn't accurate—it was really Mommy does yoga while "me" sits in a baby seat
watching), maybe stop at the farmers market, buy fresh
strawberries, zucchini, tomatoes, and basil. Joy would
pick Honey up from school. They would talk about
Honey's day on the way home, Joy a little tired and distracted from all those hours with the baby. Softball
practice, then homework would be done. In their separate houses Joy and Sara would make dinner for their

families and nurse their babies to sleep. Joy would tell Honey to get off her iPod Touch and take a bath and get in bed with a book. In their separate houses, Joy and Sara would make tender love to their husbands.

My stomach churned like it was full of macaroni salad that had sat out too long in the sun.

The next Saturday while Bree held down the Head Hunter fort and Baby Daddy did whatever he did to avoid seeing his son, I drove Skylar to the baseball field for tryouts. I always felt a mixture of pride and anxiety when I watched him play ball. I didn't care how well he did, but he'd get really upset if he didn't perform as well as he thought he should. So whenever he went to bat, I'd hold my breath and use up a prayer that he'd score a run or at least get walked. Sometimes if he'd miss, he'd run off biting his lip, fighting back tears. I wanted to force my way into the dugout and hug him, but I sat on the bleachers planning where I'd take him for ice cream afterward instead.

I'd never been into sports no matter how much the men in my life, even my darling Scott, tried to convince me otherwise, but now I appreciated baseball—the green of the diamond, the smack of the bat, the skid in the dirt clouding to dust. I told Bree her son was the only "man" who had ever gotten me to love the game.

That day was Little League tryouts. Skylar wasn't

one of the very best players, but he was strong in the field and cared more than any kid I'd ever known. He was a little small for his age, but even as a baby he'd been built like a ballplayer. Now I watched him up at bat, feet planted, eyes alert, jaw set.

"Go, Skylar!" I shouted. *Go, baby.*

I held up my iPhone, hoping a picture wouldn't jinx the at bat. The pitcher released the ball, Skylar swung. Strike one. I bit hard on my lip and put the camera down. Another pitch. Strike two. I saw Skylar's shoulders creep up. Some crazy-handsome dad yelled, "You gotta swing if it's good now."

Where the hell was Baby Daddy? Gone like Dash. *Don't think about Dash. Don't think about his baby, the one you will never have. Be here. With Skylar.*

The pitcher was Skylar's age but twice his size. Skylar swung. *Crack.* Best sound in the world. He tossed the bat and ran like the wildfire that had charred these hills over the years. I never worried about him when he was running. Once he'd slid home so hard on his chin he'd skinned it raw and got up beaming.

I stood, clapping and shouting. With this hit and his fielding skills, he'd get on a good team, for sure. That was all he really wanted. I envied that goal, although when you were ten it probably felt as overwhelming as the things I dreamed of. But that purity—that was one reason I wanted a child so much. It would keep me out of my own head, focused only on my baby's perfect, simple needs.

When tryouts were over, Skylar and I headed back down the hill. His forehead was damp when I took off his cap to rumple his hair.

"You did great, Sky."

He smiled up at me, eyes greener against his flushed skin.

"Should we go get ice cream?"

"Yes, please."

"Two scoops?"

"With sprinkles. And gummy bears."

"For reals? What about the hydrogenated oils?"

"Don't tell Mom."

As we were getting in my yellow VW Bug, the dad who'd cheered Skylar on at bat was parked next to us. A miniature, bear-cub version of himself was waiting to climb into the truck.

"Good job," the guy said to Skylar. His voice was deep and easy.

"Thanks."

"And your mom has some nice shoes there." I was wearing my black-and-silver Nike Air Jordan high-tops with black jeans and a tank top. He flashed a smile at me, his teeth small and roundish and his lips so plush-looking you could take a nap on them.

"Thanks, but I'm his godmother. His mom's working."

"Sorry, godmama. You play basketball?"

I laughed. "No. These shoes are just for show. You know, my height gives me too much of an advantage so I have to avoid the court."

"Yeah, you're pretty much nearing eight feet—am I right?"

"Eight feet one actually, but let's keep that between us. I don't want to intimidate the other players." I heard my voice deepen. It was hard to swallow. Why was my body behaving this way? It should have been shutting down with grief. Instead it was refusing to give up.

"Of course." His irises were round and brown like a child's, filling up the white space around them. They were perhaps the biggest, brownest eyes I had ever seen. "I'm Jarell," he said. "This is Darius."

The bear cub was pouting, sticking out his belly and staring up at Skylar.

"Nice to meet you, Darius." I knelt and held up my palm to high-five him. "I'm Catt."

He reluctantly offered his hand.

"As in kitty cat?" Jarell asked, but his eyes implied another, more suggestive name.

"Some people say that." There was a tightening in my groin when he helped me up, enfolding my fingers in his.

I gripped my thigh muscles to relieve the sudden ache. It felt like my body was betraying me, cheating on my sorrow. "And this is Skylar."

"Believe me, I know this one's name." He fist-bumped Sky. "I'm trying to get you on my team. You know, I was in the minor leagues till I sustained an injury, and it's all about focus and commitment. I could see that potential in you out there."

When Skylar heard the words *minor leagues,* his eyes brightened. This wasn't just some wannabe baseball dad.

"Can I take his picture with you?" I asked Jarell. "Is that okay with you, Sky?"

Skylar did that thing he does where he tries not to smile but it almost busts out anyway. I took that as a yes. Jarell put his arm around him with the confidence of a celebrity humoring a (really cute) fan, and I snapped the picture and showed it to them.

Jarell patted Skylar's Dodgers cap. "Why so serious, young man?" This brought the full smile out. "That's better. Too bad we didn't get that in the picture. Remember, baseball is serious business, but it's okay to have fun, too, you hear me?"

Sky nodded.

"I can't hear you, though." Jarell bent down, put his ear near Skylar's mouth. "What did you say?"

"Okay."

"Okay. That's better. We'll have to work on that. I'll see you around." Jarell winked at me, then strapped mini-him into his car seat and walked around to the front of the truck with the stride of an athlete and someone whose body had always been his ally. I wish I had that. It was why I went to Body Farm so often, but that confidence always seemed to elude me. What would it be like to sleep with a man like that? Would his strength rub off on me? Shoot inside?

"So he's one of the coaches? What do you think of

him?" I asked Skylar as we drove down the hill toward ice cream with sprinkles and gummy bears.

I could see his face in the rearview mirror, the dreamy look. "Cool," he said, my man of few words and expressive eyes.

After ice cream, I ordered Sky pizza, we watched Harry Potter and he took a bath. Then he got into bed in the futon in my office, the room I had always imagined would be my baby's nursery. I had spent one whole weekend painting it a pale blue with white moldings and a mural of clouds on the ceiling. Dash had come in to find me on a ladder in my old, white painter's jumpsuit and frowned. "Isn't that kind of twee?"

"What do you mean? It's for a *baby*."

At least he hadn't said, "There's no baby, Catt." Instead: "But you know, if someone else comes to stay. It's not exactly versatile."

"It's a blue sky and clouds, Dash. Everyone likes sky."

Even though Sky read to himself most nights, that night he wanted me to read a Percy Jackson book aloud to him. It was later than he usually went to bed and his eyes shut after a few pages. I drew the covers over him and kissed his cheek. His skin, like his Hawaiian dad's, was smooth and glowing, as if the sun had fallen in love with him, and his eyelashes spiked shadows across the planes of his cheekbones, his breath lifting and lowering his chest where his perfect, ever-vigilant heart slept.

"If I could pick the perfect godmother, it would be you," he mumbled.

"I love you, Sky."

"Thank you," he said. "I love you, too."

"Thank you."

"Will you stay for a little while?"

"Of course." I lay down next to him with my feet dangling off the side of the bed because I still had my Jordans on.

A little while later he whispered, "Catt?"

"Yes, sweetie?"

"You can go now because I'm technically asleep."

"Okay, baby."

Thank God Sky was there. Making me smile in the dark. Keeping at bay the ghosts that danced in the old Doc Martens Dash had left behind.

#3

When Cyan came to the door the next morning, it was raining. It rarely rains in Los Angeles, and there is a certain dirty-sweet smell that rises off the sidewalk, which accompanied him. He wore a wet, deep blue hoodie that matched his eyes and reminded me of the famous raincoat in that old, old Leonard Cohen song. In stature and with his shaved head, Cyan was so like Dash that I took a step back.

"Catt."

"Cyan."

We stood staring at each other for a few seconds before I gained enough composure to invite him in.

Tears pricked at me, fighting for an entryway, and I inhaled them back. "Why are you here?" I finally said.

He shifted his stance and shook raindrops off his shoulders. "I was just in town. For some work." I knew he had spoken to Dash. "May I sit down?"

I apologized and offered him coffee or orange juice, told him I was about to make pancakes for Sky. When I had people to care for, it helped me forget myself. Cyan only wanted green tea.

"You sure I'm not disturbing you?" he asked, when I offered him a seat at the kitchen table.

"No, it's fine. Sky's happy watching cartoons with the cat. You've met him before. My friend Bree's son?" Skylar had been staying over when Cyan visited a couple of times.

"Your godson?"

"Exactly. He's definitely sent from God."

As if on cue, Sky appeared in the doorway in Spider-Man pajamas and slippers. I gave him a hug; he always seemed to fit perfectly into my arms. "Hungry? They're almost ready. Remember Cyan?"

Sky stared at him.

Cyan nodded. "Nice to see you, Skylar."

"Hi. Auntie Catt, can I eat breakfast while I watch TV?"

"Sure. I'll bring it to you when it's ready."

He shuffled out.

"He's staying with you? Where's his mom and dad?"

"It's just some nights. Baby Daddy isn't around much. Sky's mom had a date or something. I'm glad he's here."

"How you holding up?"

"So Dash told you?" I cracked an egg into a bowl. The sizzling of butter in the pan and the sunshine and the sound of cartoons, the man in the hoodie seated at my table, made everything seem normal, but it wasn't of course.

He nodded, leaning forward, squinting into my eyes with his blue gaze. For the first time I was self-conscious—no makeup, hair a mess, ratty T-shirt. I'd been too preoccupied to notice when he'd arrived. "I was coming to town for work and I called to see what was up, and he said he'd moved out. That's all I know." He took off the hoodie and his biceps—not as big as Dash's but still impressive—flexed. "You okay?"

"Great. I've got Skylar." I tried to laugh but it made the bones in my chest ache. *But what about when Sky goes home?* I was pathetic.

"You look thin. I hope you're going to have some of those pancakes?"

Thin? I wasn't thin. But I was flattered anyway, even if he really didn't mean it as a compliment. "They're just for Sky. And you if you want."

"You look too thin. Have you guys talked at all?"

I shook my head, no, and dropped some pancake batter into the frying pan. Even the sweet, buttery smell didn't give me an appetite. The husband-leaves-you-diet. "Will he talk to you about it?"

"Not really. He's very defensive. I told him he's an idiot, though. You are by far the best—"

"Don't say it." I glared at Cyan. "I can't deal with you being kind to me right now." I didn't add, *Because you look so much like him, because you are so good-looking, be-*

cause I need someone to make it better so badly. He'd never said anything that personal to me before. Well, once . . . at my wedding to his brother.

"He met someone. I had no idea. I'm such an ass-hole." I turned away from the stove, fanning my face and biting my lip. "I'm sorry, I'm sorry."

"It's okay. Don't call yourself that. Just don't." He stood up and came over to me. I could smell the lemon soap he'd used that morning.

"Tell me about you. I can't stand to talk about this anymore. There'll be tears in the batter."

Cyan was there from Seattle for a photography gig. Some bands wanted to shoot with him, and he'd booked a few head shots as well. Usually he only worked in black and white, artsy portraits and landscapes, but he came to LA every so often to pay the bills.

I hadn't spent much time with Dash's older brother. He didn't visit often and we'd only been to see him in Seattle once, when Dash had a gig there. Cyan was Dash's only living relative, but they weren't close. Dash said Cyan was a recluse, and a bit of an eccentric; I didn't know much more than that about him. I'd always secretly wondered if Dash was jealous in some way. He almost seemed to want to avoid his brother.

When I first met Cyan, we talked about Diane Arbus and Dare Wright; Bree had recently lent me both of their biographies, and I showed Cyan *Love Monster* posts I'd done on both of them. Cyan and I also talked about Cindy Sherman, whom I especially admired. Bree and I shared a love of photography, but Dash never wanted to go with us to see the exhibits, even the 1980s LA Punk that featured one of my favorite shots of all time, and a onetime header for *Love Monster*—Exene Cervenka when she was very young, arms and legs akimbo like a broken doll with black eyeliner and hacked-off hair.

The whole time Cyan and I had talked, Dash sat with his arms crossed and his brow furrowed. I rubbed his back, wanting to make him feel included, and I remember Cyan observing that, looking pleased by it maybe. Afterward I'd asked Dash why his intelligent, interesting brother was still single. I was thinking about fixing him up with Bree, who was in the off-agains with Baby Daddy and a good, if amateur, photographer herself.

"Why get tied down? He has the best job in the world photographing all those models," Dash had said with an edge to his voice that at the time I'd interpreted as jealousy of his charismatic brother, not a reflection of something lacking in me.

Thinking of the comment now made my stomach flip like the pancake in my pan.

I was relieved to see Cyan in spite of his resemblance to Dash and the memories it brought up and I didn't really want my guest to leave right away. There was something comforting about the way his body filled the small space of the bungalow, the smooth-planed, almost monastic beauty of his face.

"Where are you staying?" I asked.

"I got a motel. I'm good."

"A motel? Is that comfortable?"

"I love motels. I'm doing a photo series on them. The older and more run-down the better."

"Cool. I'd like to see them. The photos, not the motels. My sheets are nicer, I guarantee it."

The corners of his mouth pulled up slightly; he had very full lips. "I don't doubt that. It's fine. But I'm going to be checking up on you, Catt. Seriously."

"Okay," I said. "And if you need a haircut, I'm your girl. On the house."

He laughed, smoothing his fingers over his shaved head, so well shaped it looked like an Egyptian statue's. "If I ever actually need one, yes."

"Do you want to stay for pancakes?" I really wanted him to.

"No, you have company. You two need the nutrition more than I do. You better eat some. And I have to get going anyway and hit the gym early."

"The gym? Instead of pancakes?"

"I need it to de-stress. I'll take a rain check, though."

"Of course. Where are you going to work out?"

He wasn't sure so I told him about Body Farm and gave him a guest pass I'd had in my wallet for months.

His hands were cool and strong, with large, smooth nail beds and oddly flexible thumbs, and I let him hold my hand in both of his, for a moment, before he left.

#

"Dash's brother? The hot one?" Bree said when I told her. She was an hour late to pick up Skylar, so I'd fed him dinner and helped him with his homework for the next day.

"There's only one, Bree."

She had met Cyan at my wedding and flirted with him of course, telling him about her interest in photography. "I'm obsessed with an art form entirely based on light," she had said.

"And its absence," he had corrected her.

Nothing came of it; she was solid with Baby Daddy at the time. I remembered Cyan's placid expression when they were introduced, so unlike the reaction most men had to Bree, figured he was just being respectful of Baby Daddy. But that cool regard was probably another reason why Cyan had stuck in her mind. A challenge.

"Does he have a secret crush on you or something?"

I pushed her hand away—she was trying to brush my hair out of my eyes.

"What?" She pouted at me, innocent gaze, incensed mouth.

"He just wanted to see if I was okay. All you think about is—"

"Sex. Yes, I know."

This made me flash on Dash with his sex-addict meetings and I flinched. Cyan seemed so different from his brother.

"And also, why else would he have ignored me at your wedding?"

She had a point there.

Our *Love Monster*–documented, punk-rock wedding had been at Dash's friend's house in the Hollywood Hills. Dash's band played and everyone brought food, which we later called "pot bad luck" since it was basically a mess of fruit salad, hummus, guacamole, and chips with no real main course. The dessert was good, though—our favorite homemade chocolate chip cookies and a pink-and-black skull-and-crossbones cake festooned with frosting roses. The bride and groom were a Day of the Dead skeleton couple. We hung white gauze and pink twinkle lights in the trees. I wore a white satin corset dress with layers of pink and black tulle underneath that Bree had designed and made. Bree with her artist's eyes and hands also went downtown at dawn to buy a truckload of pink and white peonies, and calla and Stargazer lilies, at the flower mart, arranged them in her collection of pretty wine bottles, put my hair in a pompadour, and did my makeup all cat's eyes and pink and white glitter. Very Adele, although no one had heard of her yet. (When she came on the scene I was happy to have a beauty icon I could identify with.) Cyan was the photographer that night and didn't really talk to anyone. But I remembered him coming into the dressing room where I was applying my pale pink frosted lipstick.

"May I photograph you now?" he said in the mirror. "The light is perfect."

I turned to him, smiling. The picture is still my favorite—my eyes bright with hope, lips parted with anticipation.

"Catt?" I turned to him. "Your face is so full of love. It's like you can see the love in everything." I didn't want to acknowledge it at the time, but the way he had said that, the way he looked at me, there was something more there, more than what was in the eyes and voice of my husband when we stood in front of all our friends and said our vows. It was a cool evening above the fraught, shining city, and I hadn't been able to stop shaking throughout the entire ceremony, as if my body knew everything that was to come.

#4

"Good-looking guy, right?" Scott said.

He had gotten me to Body Farm by telling me I had to show him pictures of Skylar's tryouts. Scott and Skylar adored books, baseball, and each other (not in that order), so I knew Scott really wanted to see the pictures and would normally have come to me. But he was trying to get me to work out instead of staying home under the covers with Sasha.

The last picture was of Sky and Jarell. We'd found out that Skylar was on his team. Practice started in a few days. I had to admit that I was looking forward to it.

Rick, on the treadmill beside me, chuckled at Scott's comment. *Good-looking guy.* He and Todd were always teasing Scott about being secretly gay. It never seemed to bother him much.

"I guess so. If that's your type," I said.

Scott knew me too well to buy my playing-it-cool

attempt. He laughed, but it was weaker than his usual chuckle. "Yeah, right."

"I prefer shorter white guys with glasses," I teased him, like usual, but he didn't smile, which was a little weird. Like everything lately. To be honest I had always preferred tall, bald guys with tattoos, but at least one of them wasn't any good for me.

"You mean Harry Potter?" Rick said.

We told Scott he looked like Daniel Radcliffe. He insisted people had always said Johnny Depp.

"Abs now, Rickster."

"Aww, Scotty, really?"

"You need to get that six-pack going."

"Let's see yours," I teased Scott. "Show us how they're supposed to look."

"Yeah," Rick chimed in.

Scott shook his head. "Nah. I'm not in the best shape right now."

What? That wasn't like Scott. He always enjoyed the opportunity to show off his muscles. I frowned at him but I didn't say anything. My head felt a little light. Maybe I just needed water? Or to go home and get in bed. Try to touch myself while fantasizing about Skylar's new coach, use him to keep visions of Dash away.

Rick finished his set and huffed off.

"Hey, Catt." Scott reached for my wrist and I stopped the treadmill, wiped sweat from my face with a towel, and turned to him. There were dark circles under his eyes, just visible beneath the rim of his Harry Potter glasses.

"You okay?" I asked. But I asked too casually, I know that now. Hindsight is twenty-twenty, but what good does it do you?

"Yeah, I think I'm coming down with something. It's no big deal. I wanted to talk to you."

I was always so comfortable around Scott, but for some reason I felt the desire to back away. "Sure. What is it, honey?"

"I just . . . I really want you to have everything you deserve," he said. "I want you to be happy."

"Thanks, Scotty. Me, too."

"No, seriously."

"Okay. You sure you're okay, though?"

"Yeah," he said. "I'm fine. I'll be fine."

"I'm going to make you some Chinese soup with lots of ginger and garlic. Can you come by tomorrow?"

"Thank you. And then maybe I can show you my new space." Scott had moved out of his girlfriend Emi's apartment a few weeks earlier. I still didn't quite understand why he had broken up with her. They'd met when she applied for a job as a trainer at Body Farm, although she'd turned it down because she didn't want to work for Big Bob. She was only in her midtwenties and Scott had alluded to some sexual issues between them. I didn't know if she was just shy and inexperienced or if it was something with Scott. In some ways he was a mystery to me. Not that I thought he was gay, but it felt like he was hiding a part of himself, holding himself back. We had flirted when we first met at Body Farm, he was my best friend besides Bree, we loved each other, but there was always this distance. And it had grown worse in the last year. I'd thought it was Emi, but now that they'd broken up, he was just as remote, if not more so.

Big Bob was at the door with the hot new girl. Her name was Leila Reynolds; Scott had introduced us. He had been training her at first, until Bob saw her and decided she was his. I wondered if Dash's new girlfriend looked like that, except with tattoos and piercings probably. "Looking good, Catt," Bob said. "Losing some weight there?"

He hardly ever talked to me. I stared at him blankly. "Thanks."

"Tell Bree to come see me," he said.

Something about him reminded me of taxidermy—the sewn back face-lift, the dead glass eyes. I realized that without Dash I was much more afraid of just about everything and everyone, which made no sense. I told myself then that I should have been afraid of Dash all along.

The next night Scott came by for soup and homemade spring rolls, which we ate on the couch, sitting cross-legged facing each other, wearing our socks. We hung out awhile and then drove over to Scott's new apartment. It was just a studio in a French Normandy building on Franklin, and he'd sold almost all of his furniture. I asked him why he'd downsized so dramatically.

"It's a fresh start. I need to be ready for change."

"What kind of change?" I asked. "You're not going on some big trip without me or something, are you?"

"Maybe." He smiled and walked over to me, his hands in his sweatpants pockets. "But it won't be forever."

Scott was a big homebody so I had no idea where he'd go. His family lived in Ohio but he rarely visited them. He didn't get along with his dad (who was sure Scott was a "queer, living out West with the queers, the Jews, and the Mexicans"), and he worried that if he had too much contact with his mom, she would have to deal with her husband's anger. Scott had told me how much he worshipped her, though. I'd seen pictures and we'd talked on the phone once or twice when I was over visiting him; she looked like a mom in a TV show and had written a bestselling vegetarian cookbook called *Corn Fed*.

"Scott," I said, "did I do something wrong? I already blew it once with Dash. I can't lose you, too."

He put his hand on my shoulder. It had been a while since he'd touched me and I calmed down immediately, the way Pinkie used to when I pet her, before the seizures started. "Of course not. You're perfect. Dash was a loser. I love you. End of story."

"So what do you mean about going away?"

"Maybe I'll go to paradise."

I kissed his cheek and he blushed where my lips brushed him. "You mean LA's not paradise?"

"Hell no."

"Yeah. Especially now," I said. And thought of Dash. Los Angeles had once been our city of quartz, of Chandleresque lakes, Didion's highways, and Westian bungalows. I'd written about it in *Love Monster* as our Garden of Eden, where wild parrots nested in flowering trees, sidewalks glittered with mica, and you could smell the ocean even all the way to the east when the winds were right. When I got sober, it was imperative that I made myself see magic everywhere, but now I was struggling to find it. Without Scott it would be even harder. "Don't you dare leave me, too."

"Well then, you have to help me make this place livable," he said. The walls were white stucco, the carpet cheap and gray. The only furniture was his futon, a table and chairs, a chest of drawers, a very small bookcase—he was using Kindle almost exclusively now. Various ashtrays reminded me of the medical marijuana Scott smoked for the pain he sometimes felt in his leg. The flatscreen TV was mounted on the wall. Scott usually had it tuned to ESPN.

"You've given everything away. How am I supposed to make it livable? Do you want to go shopping? We could get you some candles and pillows." Candles, pillows, and flowers were my solution to most problems. At least decoration problems. I wished the problem in my heart were as easy to fix. It felt like an empty room in my chest. Caving walls and splintered floors. "A cat would be nice, too."

"No. I can't take care of anybody. But I'll take Catt with a capital C and two ts. For as long as possible."

Bree had dragged me out of the house on a Thursday night. I would have much preferred to hang with Skylar while she went, but it was one of those rare occasions when Baby Daddy had him and she insisted.

The excuse of staying home and fantasizing about her son's baseball coach or crying about Dash wouldn't have worked. Even though I didn't say anything, she knew what I was thinking because she told me I needed to get a life.

"It hasn't been that long."

"Long enough. We aren't getting any younger. And you look like a widow," she said.

I felt like one. "At least I don't look as fat in black."

"You are not fat."

She wore her over-the-knee, studded boots and a T-shirt with a lavender unicorn on it. I had dyed her hair three graduated shades of light blue. Ombré, the latest trend. We pulled up in her Jeep, parked, strutted out. Or she did; I could never imitate that strut. We were going to have a few sodas, hear some music, maybe hit on a couple of guys, Bree said. I had no intention of hitting on any guys, but it wouldn't hurt to distract myself.

Bree swore to me later that she had no idea that Sliver Lake was playing at Outer Space that Thursday and I believe her, but it was too late by the time Dash came onstage. Surprise guests. I felt my dinner backing up into my throat. Bree and I had eaten tacos from a food truck.

I grabbed her wrist, digging my nails in. "We have to get out of here."

Dash—slicker than I'd ever seen him in leather pants and biker boots, shirtless on the small stage under the low ceiling. He looked like he'd been pumping iron; his abs were a neat sixer. Even as I was trying to leave, I checked around for the girlfriend; she had to be there. The strobe lights falling over me felt like eyeballs cascading from the sky. Cold air on the back of my neck. Outside there was some big paparazzi moment going on. A limo had pulled up and a girl got out. As she walked in, the lights flashed so it was hard for me to see her clearly. Just long, bare legs and a short dress that looked like it was made out of thousands of tiny silver safety pins hanging off of her collarbones and shoulders. There was so much light it hurt my eyes. I wanted to be home in the dark bungalow watching the city lights from a distance, as if I could control them, put them out with a pinch of my fingers.

"Darcy London," Bree said, nodding at the girl.

"Who?"

"The starlet du jour. That cable crime show she's on is a joke. It's called *Cold Cut* or something."

I'd heard of it; Dash had recorded a song for the sound track, but he'd told me they'd only used a tiny clip and that the show was trash.

Bree rolled her eyes. "Seriously?" she asked no one in particular, or perhaps some invisible network executive.

It was such a hot night, way too hot for April. The cruel month. The brief rain that had brought Cyan to my door was over, and you could smell the fires that were raging through the hills. Burnt brush and possibly flesh. They'd evacuated the museum on the hill that day. I wondered casually about all the art. And the animals. Sometimes fire drove wild things down into our yard. My yard. Once Dash saw a coyote watching him through the glass of the back door. Leering at me, he'd said. I wondered if animals leered or if it was only people.

When Bree dropped me off (she was going to meet her latest conquest, the Vampire, who had been elevated to semiboyfriend status), I wanted to open all my windows, but thoughts of Mandy Merrill and Adrienne Banks made me keep the windows locked. The rooms steamed like a glass hothouse. I undressed, took out my pink Rabbit vibrator, put on my headphones, and pretended Skylar's coach, Jarell, was there with me. I lay naked with my legs spread for him, touching myself, watching as he unzipped his jeans. Then he flipped me over; my ass was in the air. He was stroking me from behind, tugging on my hair, parting my lips, sinking his fingers in, prepping me, saying, "Not Kitty Cat. Maybe I'll call you Pussy, baby. My nice, juicy pussy. Man, my dick's going to like it in here." In the fantasy Dash sat on the armchair in the corner naked, watching us, jerking off. I looked up at him, squeezing my breasts and arching my eyebrows, wriggling my now small round ass for Jarell. In the fantasy Dash was pale—deathly—and he was crying with jealousy and humiliation.

The sight of him in my mind made my clit retract and it hurt to touch myself anymore. Eyes tearing with frustration, I dropped the vibrator, causing Sasha to dart out of the room, and I rolled into a ball on the bed, rubbing the insides of my thighs to alleviate the tension.

The next morning I went online to read some celebrity-gossip shit about Darcy London, as if a masochistic instinct had driven me there, so it was really my fault that I found out the way I did. If I hadn't been wasting time like that, I would still have found out, probably from Bree, but at least I wouldn't have been alone with the news. That sick feeling of falling through cyberspace by yourself. Everything there is so cold.

It was an article about Darcy London's baby daddy. She'd lost all the baby weight in two short months and looked fantastic. How did she do it? Yoga, Pilates, raw, vegan food, green-tea supplements, too! The baby had big blue eyes and a round, pale head. I just stared at the picture. Darcy London wore a pair of tight, faded cut-offs revealing the lost baby weight and a necklace made out of Barbie-doll parts over her bare chest. Her breasts were huge with milk. The baby lay in her arms like an expensive gift she had just received. I was surprised it didn't have a Tiffany blue bow stuck to its head or under its chin like a bow tie. The article said, "I'm not ready to share his name yet because when we met, he wasn't really able to commit himself fully for various reasons, but since Python's been here, well, he's just taken to fatherhood so naturally. It's a beautiful thing to watch, really. I still can't reveal who he is, but I will say that we met when he recorded a song for *Cold Cut*."

Cold. Cut. I felt a bang of blood in my head. Like I'd just had to put on the brakes to avoid running over a dog in the road. Except the dog was me. I was already run over. Dead meat. One down and eight to go would make the total of Catt's lives nine.

The baby looked like Dash.

I called Bree. "Did you see that article on Darcy London?"

She was quiet. "You saw it?"

"Yes, just now."

Silence like the line was dead. You know that feeling when a call drops and you're just talking and the other person doesn't say anything, and you think maybe they are mad at you or you said something stupid, and finally you say their name and the line is dead and you are sort of relieved and also sort of ashamed?

"Yeah," she said. "You okay?"

"So you think it's his, too?"

"Should I come over?" Bree asked. "I'm just here with Vampire Doctor but—"

"No," I said. "Really, I'd rather be alone." I couldn't see Bree. I couldn't look at anyone. My husband had never wanted a child with me; now he had found a woman he loved enough. There was no longer the possibility of denying that he was irrevocably gone

And what was more gone was our baby. The fetus curled up inside of me, his alien profile shadowy in the ultrasound photo on the refrigerator door. His new-born face scrunched against my breast. His milk-filled belly warm in a blue terry-cloth onesie, as he slept in his crib in the room painted with clouds.

This was what brought me to my knees onto the kitchen floor as if I were miscarrying.

I cried most of the night, but in the morning, when the sun shone through the same window where a coyote once lurked, I told myself it was not Dash that I had loved, as much as the idea of Dash and what I believed he could give me.

I put Dash's Docs in a bag for the Goodwill and threw his toothbrush away. I could mourn for the child that would never be, but I could no longer mourn for Dash.

I made myself meditate and eat a good breakfast. I

went early to the gym. After work I picked Skylar up and took him to practice. Bree had a late-afternoon client and was going out for happy hour after that. ("Agave-sweetened cucumber-kale lemonade only, of course.") This was good; I loved being with Skylar, and the idea of seeing his new coach wasn't too bad, either, I told myself.

But at the field Jarell looked busy with the kids so I parked and read my Frida Kahlo biography for my next *Love Monster* post while Skylar practiced. I could always spot him easily—he was one of the smaller boys, but the way he squared his shoulders and planted his feet, you could just see every cell poised in concentration. As I sat there, in the shade of the trees, trying to focus on my book and how hot Jarell looked and not on how big and cold my bed felt now, I got a text.

I'm going to be in your area tonight. Would you like to have dinner? Want to make sure you don't waste away.

My heart slammed out of the ballpark and I had to catch my breath. *Was Dash texting from another number?* Until I recognized the area code and realized it was Cyan, of course. I'd given him my cell phone number before he left.

I didn't mind the idea of sitting across from him and staring at his face while we shared a meal. He wasn't Jarell but it was for the best; I knew I wasn't in danger of getting carried away with Cyan. I wanted to distract myself with sex but it was a bad idea. When I was younger and slept around, I always ended up crying as soon as the guy was inside me and scaring him away. This was before I really had all that much to cry about.

Sure, I wrote back. *At Sky's practice. Done by 7:30. I'll cook, though.*

No, I insist. Dinner on me.

A little later the sky was turning a deep pink and Skylar came loping over, flushed, his bat bag swaying on his shoulder, way too big for him. I got out of the car and helped him put the bag in back, hoping Coach might see me and come over, but he didn't.

It's okay, you're going to see Cyan. You can ask about Dash. Stupid, Catt, stupid. You think this will change anything?

It was Bree's whole demeanor that changed when she came to pick up her son and saw my brother-in-law. Ex-brother-in-law? Her eyes got bigger, she pushed out her chest; it was a reflex with her. I was so used to disappearing around her that I just accepted it. Something was different this time, though.

"This is Cyan. Cyan, this is Bree. You've met before. At the wedding." I couldn't say *our* wedding.

Cyan shook her hand. I looked closely at his face—not a glimmer of change, let alone the sea change I was used to when she entered a space. As if he still didn't really see her. Strange.

"The photographer," she said, holding his hand an extra second, until he moved it away.

"Yes."

"You have a really good eye." Little-girl teeth and dimples.

"Thank you."

"That picture of Catt getting ready is my favorite."

"It's all your makeup, Bree," I told her. Then, to Cyan: "And good lighting and angles."

"It was all you, Catt," Cyan said, face placid.

She stood staring at him, seemingly unfazed that he wasn't playing her game. "I'd love to pick your brain about photography sometime," she said. "People have asked me to model, but I'm more interested in the other side of the camera, honestly. Sometimes I'll just model in order to learn more about taking pictures. You can learn a lot that way."

He nodded, then turned away from her chatting to me. "I made reservations at eight."

Bree's eyebrows shot up. "Oh, okay." She pulled her son against her hip as if she'd just realized he was there. He'd been busy with his iPod and didn't seem to mind either way. "Let's get going, Skylar."

"I fed him a big meal before and a snack after," I said.

"Thanks, Catt, you're the best."

I loved how Sky still threw his arms around me with abandon when we hugged, and I hoped it would continue for as many more years as possible. I pushed his still-damp hair back off his forehead, which, hidden from the sun, was a shade paler than the rest of his face. "See you soon, buddy." When I opened the door the night air, oversweet with jasmine blossoms, felt cool on my face. I was tired from the day but suddenly I wanted to go out.

Cyan drove us to Palm Latitudes, a restaurant in an old, pink adobe building; we sat in the courtyard beside a fountain, among potted palms strung with chili-pepper lights. I asked him to take some pictures of the place for my blog.

He ordered ceviche and tamales with mango salsa and I watched him across the mosaic table, thinking how much he looked like Dash, and yet how different they were. I'd only seen one childhood picture of the two brothers because Dash said his mother hardly took any to begin with and he'd thrown away the rest.

"Why?" I'd asked, and he'd said his childhood wasn't worth remembering and could we talk about something else?

I knew only that his father had died when he was three and his mother was crazy, that alcohol had killed her. That Dash and Cyan weren't that close, but that Cyan had been protective in some ways and Dash was grateful to him for that.

In the one remaining picture, Cyan pulled chubby-baby Dash and a white Siberian-husky puppy in a small, red cart.

If Dash and I had a child, he would have looked like the baby in the photo.

"You okay?" Cyan brought me out of the fantasy. "Eat your food."

A waitress walked by with a tray of beers and sangria, and I had to keep myself from staring. I was suddenly wicked thirsty and not for the mineral water he'd ordered. "Thanks. How's your work going?"

"I got some more gigs. Bands mostly. No one wants to pay much these days, though, except for weddings."

"But you're so good," I said.

He thanked me. "It's just that with digital, everything's different. People don't understand the cost."

"How'd you get into it?" I was trying hard not to think about Dash anymore.

"Taking pictures as a kid, nonstop. I guess I got into it the way any artist starts doing art—to make the world look the way you want it to. Like in your blog. Isn't that why you do hair, too?"

I laughed. "Well, I don't know if it's an art. And no. It's to make people feel better."

He scanned my face, tapping his cleft chin with his index finger. There was a slight growth of stubble. "Of course it is. I forgot who I was talking to for a second. The caretaker." No sarcasm edged his voice.

"You should know. Why else would you be feeding me like this, checking up on me?"

He shook his head no. "It's for selfish reasons. I don't want to lose my only sister. Free haircuts and everything."

"You don't really need much hair care." I reached to touch his polished-smooth scalp but decided against it. *Inappropriate, Catt.* "I thought we'd established that."

"Too true. The male-pattern-baldness shave I can do myself. But still."

We made small talk for the rest of the evening, and I almost got away without asking about Dash, even after the "not losing me" comment. Got away with not asking, that is, until Cyan drove me home. I couldn't help it; I invited him in and we sat at the kitchen table drinking tea from the Botanic Garden patterned cups he'd bought for our wedding present. A Björk song came on, "All Is Full of Love." That did it.

"Okay. What did Dash say?"

Cyan rubbed his eyes with his fists. Tired. "Good song."

"The best. Not to mention the Björk-bot video. I posted it on *Love Monster* once."

"I was wondering if you were going to ask."

It took me a moment to remember what we'd been talking about. Björk was an easier topic. "I tried not to."

"He's an asshole, Catt, I'm sorry. I know he's my brother, but he's screwing it up."

I looked away, feeling the tears again. *Damn.* "I don't understand why."

"I don't think he does, either. Fear? I don't know. Cliché alert here. But you were the best thing that ever happened to him, seriously."

"No. He was. To me." I'd been safe, it seemed. Not anymore.

Cyan sat quietly for a while, long fingers wrapping the mug with the purple and white passionflowers on it. *Passiflora caerulea.* My cup had the pink-blossomed virgin's-bower vine clambering around its circumference.

"What should I do?" I blurted.

"Just take care of yourself. The way you do with everyone else. He'll come back or he won't, but either way you'll have you. Which beats the alternative."

He was right. Why hadn't I learned that? I thought of my mother, then, drinking too much, taking diet pills, not coming home until dawn, out on another date. While I lay awake in her bed that smelled of cigarettes, watching late-night TV, eating cornflakes for dinner. Telling myself, *You'll never be this kind of mother.* Never going to be any kind of mother, now. But I had Skylar. I needed to "have me" for him.

Cyan rubbed his eyes again and yawned. "Damn, I'm about to pass out. Can I just take a catnap on your couch for, like, ten minutes before I go?"

"Of course." I said. It was comforting to have him around anyway.

An hour later he was still fast asleep, with Sasha sitting on his chest as if she were trying to get him to stay there forever, and I couldn't bring myself to wake him. His feet hung off the edge of the couch, vulnerable in very clean white socks, his boots placed neatly beside him. I covered him with a blanket, studying the hard, symmetrical angles of his face. *You were the best thing that ever happened to him.* Was it possible that Cyan . . . ? No. Impossible. He had called me his sister. He just cared about me. Why couldn't I just let a man care and not try to turn it into more?

I got in bed with my laptop, feeling a little dejected without my cat, and googled Cyan Berns.

I'd seen his shots of Dash's band, of course, and Dash had showed me his brother's website a long time ago, but I hadn't thought about it much, except to agree that it would be great if he could photograph our wedding. Now the images looked different to me—clues into the mind of the photographer. Moody shots of run-down motels and abandoned fairgrounds that infused the rotting structures with a beauty they'd never had before. Close-up, color shots of flowers that had been soaked in liquid nitrogen and shattered into fragments. Black-and-white portraits of musicians and models. I couldn't help it; I looked for Dash. And there he was—an old shot, when he was thinner and still drinking and using. Growling into the mic, his face contorted with shadows. Was she there in the audience—"her"? Had she been watching him, waiting all this time? Of course not. If she'd wanted him, she'd have had him. And she was too young; she probably wasn't old enough to get into a club back then. I clicked back to the models. Their eyes looked preternaturally big, limbs deerlike, their mouths slightly open, long, wet hair streaming down over their chests. They were thin and perfect. I was an idiot.

#

I woke a few hours later to a loud sound outside, like someone crashing into a metal trash can. Before I knew what I was doing, I had bolted from the bed and was creeping to the living room. Cyan stood at the window in the dark, looking out. A tall silhouette against the dark leaf patterns beyond the glass. Relief at seeing him was like liquor in my blood. If I had been alone, whom would I have called? Who would have come if I just said I'd heard a noise?

He turned to me, his finger to his lips, and relief became embarrassment mixed with a tingling feeling in my nipples; I wasn't wearing a bra.

"Do you have an alarm?" he asked me, looking back outside. His voice was only a whisper.

"It's not working. Dash didn't think we needed it anymore."

"I think you should get it working," he said.

"What was that sound?" I shivered and my feet cringed against the wooden floorboards.

"I'm going to go look."

"Maybe we should call the cops," I said, alarmed by the weight of his voice.

"I'll just look around a little."

Cyan shoved on his boots without sitting down and opened the glass doors. "Lock this behind me, okay?"

I did as I was told. Stayed in the same place, gripping the edge of the couch where Cyan had slept, listening to my heartbeat exposed bralessly under the thin, vintage Siouxsie and the Banshees T-shirt. Felt like I waited forever. I heard Cyan hissing at something and the sound of twigs breaking and scuttling leaves.

When he came back in, I forgot to cover my chest at first. "So, it was a cat?" I asked. *Or maybe a coyote?*

"Get an alarm," Cyan evenly said.

I got back in bed but couldn't sleep so I jammed my hand between my thighs and tried to rub away the tension of the night as I thought of Skylar's hot baseball coach licking me. Cyan's face appeared in my mind just as I came. I slept fitfully after that.

Cyan had to hit the road the next morning, after a cup of green tea and a promise to send me the pictures of Palm Latitudes for *Love Monster;* he had some photography jobs in Santa Barbara.

"Get an alarm," he said again before he left. "I'll check in to make sure you do, okay?"

At work I told Bree about the sound I'd heard in the night. I didn't mention that Cyan had stayed over.

"So you're not sure what it was?" she said.

"Maybe an animal. It really freaked me out, though." Stu had come in for his buzz and was watching us so I lowered my voice. "With those killings, and Dash gone . . . I guess I'm more jumpy than usual. I called the alarm company. Maybe I'll finally get another dog." But the guilt was too much. Pinkie would have protected me to the death. And I had basically killed her.

"Do you want to stay with us tonight?" Bree asked.

"No. I'll be okay. You should get an alarm system, too, though." Bree and Skylar only lived a short distance from me.

"Excuse me, ladies, I don't want to interrupt your convo, but I have a meeting at noon in the Valley," Stu said, cracking his knuckles. I guess he had heard me after all. "And *I'm* the one who's obsessed with that serial killer?"

#5

A week later Stu was back. "Where's Bree?" he said, not looking at me.

"She called in sick. Didn't she let you know?"

"Aw, fuck." He spun on his heel. Then he turned back around and ran a hand over his scalp. His arms were too short but his hands were big and dangled from his wrists. "You want to give it a shot?"

While I was buzzing him, Stu told me about a new show he was producing called *Hook Up,* where the audience got to choose which contestants would sleep together.

"Bree should come on it," he said. "That woman is so hot. Must be tough, huh? You must hear it all the time."

I didn't say anything.

"Although maybe there are some guys who aren't into skinny women with big tits and flawless skin."

"Excuse me?"

The news was on. Stu picked up the remote and hit

the volume. A solemn female newscaster with a dimpled baby face and a deep voice was standing in front of the HOLLYWOOD sign as words appeared on the screen: *Hollywood Serial Killer's Third Strike?*

"This is the third mutilated female body that's been found in this area. Police still have no leads. . . ."

When I'd heard about the ones before, I'd had hope to distract me—my husband, my desire for a child. That day I had only pain from which to be distracted.

How could someone kill and mutilate? As if these women were things? Pieces of bloody trash. I felt that way myself. I didn't want to admit it, it sounded self-important, narcissistic. What Dash had done to me was nothing like this. But somehow it brought up that tossed-aside-ness, that vicious severing.

"I wonder what he did to this one?" Stu's said. His voice sounded like he was biting the inside of his lip. "Arms, legs. Maybe head this time?" It was like I wasn't there. Then I wondered if I'd imagined him saying it?

The chill that went from the nape of my neck down my arms to my hands was not just from the cold air blasting out of the vent. In spite of it the armpits of my T-shirt were soaked through with sweat. A girl's face appeared on the screen. Wide-eyed, tan, and full-mouthed like the others.

"The victim has been identified as Michelle Babcock, an aspiring actress and model. She was from Indiana and had come to Los Angeles to pursue her career while attending USC. She had last been seen after class leaving the USC campus, where she was studying library science."

It was my neighbor Skipper.

Library science? I hadn't even asked her what her name was.

It's not easy to fuck up a buzz cut, but I did it, nicking Stu's brick-shaped head. His hand whipped out at me and I stepped back so he didn't make contact.

"Bitch. What the hell?"

"Sorry." *Fuckface.* Mascara-tainted tears stung my eyes.

"They should fire your ass. What's wrong with you? If Bree wasn't working here, no one would even come around." He got up and walked out without paying me.

I, or someone who had hijacked my body, shouted after him, "Good luck with Bree. She wouldn't fuck you to save her life."

I wanted to walk down to the corner liquor store and bring back a bottle of Jack; I could almost taste the burn. Instead I called Bree and our sponsor, Shana, but they didn't pick up. When I got home, there was a message from Dash, who had heard about Michelle Babcock. I erased the message before it was over; I couldn't hear his voice. Not when I was alone in the night in what had once been our home, not after what had happened to Michelle. So I called Bree again and this time she answered.

"Oh my God. Your neighbor. Are you okay? Do you want to stay with us for a while?" I could imagine her twisting her lilac-streaked hair around her fingers the way she did when she was anxious, trying to soothe herself.

"I'm okay. Stu didn't help, though."

"What a fucker. Don't listen to him."

She asked me again if I wanted to stay there, at least for one night, but I told her no. I didn't want to leave the house again. When she hung up, I googled Michelle Babcock to see if there was anything about her that might explain why this had happened. The only thing I could see was that she looked a little like the other two women and that they were all model/actresses. Why hadn't I gotten to know her? Did she have friends in LA? A boyfriend? I'd never seen her jogging with anyone. How alone had she been? What had she felt when that man, whoever he was, had clamped his hands onto her in the dark?

When I couldn't think about it anymore, I checked my Facebook page. There was a message from Jarell Hardin. His profile revealed the team he'd played for in the minors, that he was male and single. That he was interested in baseball, music, poetry, yoga, meditation. There were pictures of him coaching, scowling in a hoodie, smiling in a suit, playing baseball, cheering at a Dodgers game, holding a baby, hugging the same child a few years later, both of them serious, staring with round, brown eyes.

How did anyone hook up before the Internet?

Especially if you didn't go to bars and get wasted. It was so easy online.

Thanks for making my day with your smile and your Jordans, he had written.

Thank you for being so cool to Skylar.

He responded right away. *He's a great kid. With a hot godmother.*

My body contracted gently. *And a very, very hot coach, Coach.*

Nice, he messaged.

Truth, I messaged back.

Hey, we need some face time soon. I'd like to get to know you better.

Sounds good.

Even Bree, who slept with a lot of guys, would not have approved. I hardly knew him at all. And he was Skylar's coach. But I told myself that made him a good guy, probably, and Little League was a better and safer reference than FU Cupid, especially with what was going on out there in the streets. Besides, I knew how to keep my relationships with men separate from my love for Skylar. And Jarell had come into my life at exactly the right time.

At that point even if I thought he was dangerous, I might have decided it was worth it. The possibility dangled by that monster, Love, was better than the slow agony of psychologically hemorrhaging to death alone. And now that Cyan was gone and my neighbor was dead, I'd probably be safer with Jarell in my bed than without him anyway.

Not to mention, I needed all the comfort I could get. And sex was comfort. Short of drinking, which I knew I couldn't do, it was the quickest way I knew to feel better, at least for a while.

Jarell looked even taller in my house. He probably had at least three inches on Dash and was much leaner, but I was used to seeing Dash crammed in there. Jarell—everything about him was big: eyes, nose, lips, hands, feet. He bent down to hug me lightly. He smelled like weed and, maybe, shea butter? Some expensive and natural cream. I did not believe at all in the sending of angels, but if I did, I would have thought he was one.

I offered him some sparkling water, which I brought in and poured in the best wineglasses with the gold rims. He sat on the couch, which looked like playhouse furnishing.

I joined him and we clinked and sipped the water. Up this close he resembled a movie star; his features were so symmetrical it made me uneasy.

"I hope you don't mind just having water."

"No, that's cool. That's cool."

"So Skylar's doing okay so far?" I asked.

Jarell leaned forward, legs spread, elbows on knees,

and looked at me sideways. "Yeah, he's doing good. He's a good kid. A little hard on himself, but, yeah."

"He really loves baseball. It's this total passion."

"Yeah. It's a tough road, though. You know, I was in the minors. It was all I thought about, all I did. Well, almost." His gaze was predatory.

There were more things I had wanted to ask him—about his career, his childhood, the interests listed on his Facebook page, his son, Skylar—but everything had flown out of my head.

"Is this your mala?" Jarell pointed out my beads in a gauze bag. I'd moved them into the living room one day but hadn't actually used them. "Do you meditate?"

"I should more often," I said. To be honest I hadn't meditated since the morning after I'd read about Darcy London's baby. In spite of my early interest in rosaries, I guess maybe it was Dash who'd been the spiritual one in the family. Or at least he knew how to appear that way. "Do you?" Of course I knew the answer from stalking Jarell's Facebook page.

"It helps me stay cool. But the room's heating up right now." He finished his water, held out his glass, and I refilled it.

"If I knew this morning that the hottest man I'd ever seen was coming over, I'd have picked up something else besides Perrier."

"The hottest?" He frowned at me. "Who you talking about?"

I shook my hair out of my eyes (it still smelled vaguely like hot metal from the flatiron) and met his. "Who do you think?"

He flashed his best head-shot smile. "Okay, well, I hope you're telling me the truth because otherwise none of it matters."

"Okay, maybe not the hottest ever, but the hottest I've seen up this close."

"Now that I'll take." Jarell leaned over and kissed me on the lips. His were twice the size of mine. "How's that?" he asked.

I grabbed his face and pulled him into me. We were mad kissing, or I was; his mouth was slow, not urgent. I felt his hands on my waist and I only had a second to worry about the flesh there before he had hoisted me onto his lap, his hands on my ass. The way he did that wasn't slow or calm at all, though his mouth seemed almost lazy. I felt his hardness pressing up against me, and it made me shiver so much it was a convulsion.

"You like the feel of that?" he whispered.

He moved me aside slightly and unzipped his shorts, took out his cock. It was huge and I stopped kissing him to stare at it. Perfect. No wonder his last name was Hardin. I got down on my knees on the wooden floor and put my hands on his inner thighs.

"You like that?" he asked.

I nodded dumbly and my mind stuttered. I put my lips softly on him and he shuddered. I bent my head and took just the tip in my mouth, swirling my tongue around the groove, starting to suck. I wondered how much of him I could fit inside me.

"Slow down, Kitty Cat. If you're not careful with that juicy mouth, I might come right into it."

I looked up at him, through my lashes. "Don't you want to?"

"Not yet." He adjusted himself and hauled me up so my legs were straddling his cock. My panties were thinner from dampness and I could feel him pressing into me. Damn.

"I don't have a condom," he whispered. "I didn't think this would happen when I came over. I don't want you to think—"

"It's okay," I said. "But neither do I."

"Then I'm getting one." He moved me off of him and stood up, zipping his shorts. He leaned over and kissed me once on the lips. "Don't move from there. I'll be right back."

When Jarell returned from the store and kissed me again, in that same lazy way, his mouth tasted of weed, good weed.

He put his hands on my hips. "Where are we going to do this?"

I turned and he followed me to the bedroom, the mattress I'd bought new when Dash and I met. I hadn't slept with anyone else on it. My body was tensing up as I looked at that bed and I was thinking of the smell of the weed. The taste, too; it was still on my mouth.

"Mind if I smoke?" Jarell asked, taking out a joint. I lit candles while he fired up. "Want some?"

Maybe one puff wouldn't hurt. I wasn't a drug addict anyway; alcohol had always been my thing. It had never led to drinking, had it? They were very different sensations. Weed just made me sleepy normally. It had been a long time. I wanted the ease and grace I imagined it could give me, like Jarell's grace.

No, Catt. Maybe a contact high, though. Shit. You need to call Shana in the morning.

I politely declined the weed, but told him he was welcome to smoke. Then I fell back on the pillows. Rihanna was singing and I closed my eyes to disappear into her voice as he fell on top of me.

"Your pussy's so wide-open." There was a reverence in his voice but it also made me feel a little sick, as if he thought something wasn't quite right about that, not quite normal. Too easy.

I tried to stroke his head but the gesture felt overly intimate, as if I were holding his brain, so I put my hands on his shoulders. They were more delicate-feeling than they appeared, though broad. Compared to Dash, Jarell's whole body was fine, not bulky. But his cock was both long and thick and it pressed against the engorged place inside of me while his pelvic bones massaged my clit. As I came, first from outside, in small, tight spurts of pleasure, and then deep and convulsively from within, I floated up out of my body and watched us fucking below. I wondered if that was the perspective you achieved right before you died. Had Michelle Babcock seen her body this way after she left it?

When it was over, he threw himself aside and lay sprawled out across the bed diagonally. His limbs were so long and shadows darkened the indentations of muscles. There was a lotus-flower tattoo above his heart that I hadn't seen before.

After some time he asked for a washcloth and went into the bathroom. I heard him washing for a long time, rinsing me meticulously off of him. I put my fingers between my legs and sniffed; I smelled good, sweet and musky, so I didn't think that was the problem. Just a fastidious man, like a cat. He came back in.

There was a loud sound outside and I sat up.

Jarell frowned at the open windows. "Mind if I close these? With that piece of shit killing all those women out there . . ."

Mandy Merrill. Adrienne Banks. Michelle Babcock. Their faces floated up in my mind like candles and then winked out.

"The last one, Michelle, she was my neighbor." Saying it out loud made it worse.

"That's fucked-up."

After he closed the windows and came to lie beside me, I moved my body until it fit into the curve of his arm.

"You okay?" he asked.

I nodded and swallowed. I didn't want him to see me cry. When I lay my hand lightly on the flat playing field of his abdomen, he took my fingers and moved them to his groin. The hair was sparse and curly and his cock was hard.

I danced my fingertips up the shaft. "You're amazing," I said.

"My ex-wife didn't think so."

I waited for him to explain.

"She wanted what she called the finer things. The house, the car. It didn't work out that way. I love to work with kids, but it doesn't exactly pay the big bucks."

So here was the chink in the wall of this confident man. And it made me like him even more, much more.

I was already wet and swollen with more wanting. We fucked again, almost as long as the first.

"You just keep on taking more and more of me. Tell me how much you want this long, hard dick inside your dripping pussy."

"Please," I gasped. "I want it so, so bad."

This time I came more softly, in lapping, lulling waves that washed away the remaining tension in my pelvis. He fell asleep on top of the sheets beside me, on his back, penis reclining against his thighs. So unself-conscious; I could never sleep like that, even alone, but especially not in a stranger's bed. And as relaxed as I was from coming, and even with the security of having Jarell lying beside me, I couldn't shake the feeling that someone was watching us from the dark outside the window.

#

He was inside me once more, at dawn, hard as the night before, softly whispering the word *goddess* into my ear.

But I was no goddess. And something was deeply wrong. With the world. With me.

I knew I should get my ass to a fucking meeting. At least pick up my mala, meditate, and say a sobriety prayer. But the best I could manage was to answer my phone when Shana called me back on my way to work. By then she'd heard about Michelle Babcock of course and insisted that we all go to a meeting together that night. I told her that I'd thought about smoking weed with Jarell.

"I might have to fire your ass," she said. "You're going to be sharing tonight, just so you know."

As usually happened in meetings, my heartbeat sped up and it was hard to breathe. I remembered why I didn't like to go that much, hated to share.

"I'm Catt, and I'm an alcoholic."

"Hey, Catt," the room said back. The church basement smelled musty and the fluorescent lights made my head hurt, made my eyelids heavy. My butt ached on the metal folding chair. Shana was on one side of me with her long, curly, black hair and white designer, skinny jeans, and Bree was on the other.

"I have eleven years and I want to go back out." I fingered the sobriety pendant on my key chain. "All

I want sometimes is a drink. Especially after what happened to that woman. Michelle. She was my neighbor
but I never even talked to her. I'm a fucking mess. Thank
God I have my friends."

Bree squeezed my hand and I winced a smile at her.
Shana nodded, face somber.

"Thanks for letting me share," I said.

Across the room a guy was watching me. Was he?
He didn't look away when I glanced over. Typical forty-
something hipster in a fedora and sideburns. Were-
wolf. But he was handsome—square-jawed, strong face,
deep-set eyes under thickly bristling eyebrows. I thought
I remembered his name. Dave? No, Dean. He had written a cult horror novel and ran a poetry night at the
cafés. The writing was violent, poetic, like Chuck Palahn-
iuk and Sylvia Plath's love child. I thought maybe Dash
had mentioned him before.

But men in the program were off-limits. I'd already
broken that rule once with Dash and proven its valid-
ity. Besides, I had Jarell. Did I? Maybe I'd see him again,
but I wasn't sure.

During the rest of the week I worked out harder than
usual, drank a lot of vegetable juice, had Bree cut and
color my hair and got a bikini wax from Kendra at the
salon, because in our world at least, goddesses and
would-be goddesses did not have body hair.

I lay in happy-baby yoga pose, on my back, legs bent, feet in hands, on the table, and Kendra ripped the hair out of the pores, leaving me writhing. She stroked the tiny remaining patch for just a split second as if to calm me, remind me that this was a pleasure spot. All I felt was searing heat, but there was a gentle tingling where she'd touched me. Kendra's hair was back in a sleek bun. I could never pull off that look, but it enhanced the fine, strong features of her face and the silk of her skin. I envied that skin and imagined it against Jarell's, which was about one shade darker. She had a slim, strong frame with slender, muscular arms. Across her large breasts her tight T-shirt said TAKE IT ALL OFF.

Kendra was one of those people who radiated happiness with a vengeance. She took acting classes and dance classes, ran marathons, hiked in the mountains, went camping, read all the bestsellers, saw all the latest movies, and cooked gourmet dinners. She had told me once that happiness was the entire reason to be alive, and she considered the pursuit of it her ongoing project.

"Your skin is so sensitive," she said. "You'll need lots of cortisone and aloe and some antibacterial lotion until it calms down."

"Okay," I gasped, trying not to scream. Was she done yet? She told me to put the soles of my feet together and pull the skin on my belly taut. Oh, God, not the lips. "I don't think I really want a full Brazilian," I said.

"Too late. Sorry."

You free tonight? Jarell texted me as if he had a sixth sense for waxed V's. It was the first time I'd heard from him except for a brief thank-you text after he'd left that morning and the chaste hug he'd given me when I dropped Skylar off at practice. (I'd seen him hug a few other moms this way, too.) I texted right back, refusing to play Bree's hard-to-get game.

I just got super-waxed. Sore.

I can make it better.

I kissed him at the door and it turned deep fast, and he pulled away and said, "You're ready to go. I like that about you, Kitty Cat. No games."

I worried again that this was a bad thing—that I was too easy, that I should have waited. But it was too late, and besides, I wanted him. He was right; I was ready to go.

As soon as we were in the bedroom, he had a hit of weed, then pulled off my T-shirt, unhooked my red lace bra, threw it aside, and stared at my naked breasts. They felt full and achy, needing to be touched. I pressed my forearms against the flesh to ease the growing pressure.

His erection was tenting his shorts. He pulled off his clothes, still staring at me. "Take off your pants," he said. "Take off your panties. I want to see this sore pussy."

Instantly even wetter, I ripped open the button fly of my cutoffs with one hand and stepped out of them; then before I could slide off my underpants, he grabbed me and pulled the panties off. He laid me down on the bed and gently spread open my legs with his knee. I wanted to hump that big knee, have him press it against my pelvis where the tension was building so fast it felt explosive.

I handed him a bottle of aloe by the bed. "She told me to use this."

Jarell massaged the cool gel into my skin, his fingers lightly grazing my clit as if by accident. I thought briefly of Kendra's fingers there.

"Is that better, baby?"

Baby? Goddess? I reached up, put one hand on his neck and brought his lips to mine. His tongue licked my mouth the way he kissed me between my legs, firm and slow, steady. He ripped open the condom packet and rolled one on, flipped me over so he was on his back, I was on top. My eyes opened wide.

He was staring at me, smiling. "Went right in," he said. "How's your sore pussy? Okay?"

"Now it is," I said, clenching around him. Maybe it was from all the blood down there, the contrast to the pain, or maybe it was the "baby," but I came harder than before, clinging onto his neck until he shot into me. "Fuck fuck fuck."

Before he left, he asked me if I was going to be the one taking Skylar to the game on Sunday.

Baby. Goddess.

I realized I was thinking like a teenager, basing all my self-worth on the offhand comments of a man I didn't even know. Arrested development of the addict. But I couldn't seem to stop.

"Yes," I told him.

I sat on the bleachers watching Skylar and the kids play baseball, Jarell standing on the field throwing hand signals, all those little faces turned to him with complete trust. He looked so tall next to them. I couldn't see his eyes under his baseball hat.

In the hills above the park something was prowling. "Look," the parents said. A mountain lion was walking along the ridge, watching us. The sun was setting, and the sky was streaked with pink and orange. The air smelled fiery, mixed with the grease smells of the hot dog stand. I wanted everyone to get out of there. Once I'd read you were supposed to make yourself really big if you encountered one of these cats head-on, so the mountain lion wouldn't think you were a small animal. The Little League team looked like puppies from where I sat.

Jarell came over to the fence. "It'll be okay," he said. "Someone just called animal control."

The parents were laughing nervously; the kids were

pointing at the creature, distracted from the game. Jarell clapped his hands and they snapped to attention.

His team won by one run and the puppy boys jumped all over their coach.

I felt shy but I made myself go over to him later. I couldn't see his face, shadowed by his hat, but he smiled at me, conveying secrets with his teeth. His body blocked the setting sun, dark shoulders against the sky. Someone had come for the mountain lion. I smelled smoke.

Jarell's son, Darius, came over, pulling on his father's T-shirt. "Daddy, I want fries and Gatorade."

"Water and pretzels."

"Hi, Darius," I said. "Great game, huh?" The little boy frowned at me and asked for fries again.

I felt a tugging in my chest. What would a child of mine and Jarell's look like? Chocolate-milk skin, green eyes, soft, loose curls. My belly tightened along with my chest muscles.

"Just a minute. I'm talking to my friend Catt," Jarell said to his kid, firm but gentle, which is how he touched me in bed. I remembered him sliding in with one movement the other night.

But then he hugged me lightly, as if I were a small child, something delicate and precious, although his eyes on me were like big, plundering hands. "Thanks for coming," he said, and then, more softly, "Do I get to see you soon? Where we're the only wild animals."

#

The last time Jarell and I were together, he lifted me onto his hips and stalked over to the mirror as if I hardly weighed a hundred pounds and watched our reflection as he bounced me up and down on him.

"Look," he said. I was afraid to see my big, white ass. "Look," he said again.

"I'm scared."

"Why?"

"It's too much." I realized I wasn't only scared of my big ass; I was scared of having this image in my mind. Because I would want to hold on to it then, I would want it to happen again and again. I would see it in the dark every time I closed my eyes and I would want it to return in the bouncing, pounding flesh. But at least it might obliterate the faces of Mandy Merrill and Adrienne Banks.

I went on Jarell's Facebook page after he left and saw that he was tagged in a picture with his arm around a young woman at a ball game. Blond braids and candy-blue eyes, fake breasts, henna tattoos on her hands. This was how a goddess looked in 2013. What did I expect?

Doubt has cold fingers and they can rip you open and creep right under your skin.

Doubt, that bitch, was what got me to tell Bree about Jarell at work the next day. I'd kept my secret from her this long because I knew what she was going to say.

I was right. Bree shook her head at me in the mirror as she fixed her lipstick. At least she didn't chastise me for screwing her son's coach. She knew that I'd never let my feelings for Jarell affect Skylar in any way. "You mean he's never even taken you out?"

"We stayed in. It's what I wanted." Not sounding defensive at all, of course.

"But he didn't take you out afterwards? He hasn't even bought you a coffee?"

I wanted to suggest that maybe he had to pay his ex-wife a lot of alimony, but I stopped myself. I was sounding pathetic. I had no idea what the deal was with Darius's mother. Jarell and she could even still be together, for all I knew, in spite of what Facebook said.

"I hate to be harsh, but it's just a booty-call situation, Catt."

"Yeah," I said. "I know."

"I mean, if that's what you want, it's fine. God knows I've gone for those. Especially if he's hot enough."

"He is."

"But you're in a vulnerable position with everything that's happened." I was grateful to her for not saying Dash's name out loud. Or bringing up Michelle Babcock. "Well, if he calls you within the week and asks you to dinner, I think it's awesome, but if not, I think you should break it off."

And that was what I did. He didn't call but he texted at seven forty-five the next Saturday night asking if he could come over. *Booty call,* I thought. I didn't reply.

That night I dreamed that while I gave him head, on my hands and knees on the mattress, he slid his finger into my ass, pulling me back and pushing me forward like a sucking machine.

When Bree sent me a link to FU Cupid, I signed up.

I took Skylar to his game; I had made a pact with myself that my dalliance would never interfere with his happiness. Unfortunately, it didn't exactly work that way.

Maybe Skylar picked up the tension from me or maybe he was just having a bad day, but after he struck out the second time he hung his head and I knew he was crying as he ran to the dugout. In the next inning Jarell put him on third and he tagged a kid on the opposing team who was declared safe. It was hard to tell if the kid had really made it or not. Skylar was angry; I saw that clearly, though.

On his third at bat I held my breath, sick to my stomach, praying for him to at least make contact. I hadn't been praying enough lately, I realized. Might as well use one on my favorite person on the planet.

But he struck out again, and this time when he ran off, he was crying. I wanted so badly to go to him in the dugout, but I knew it was off-limits. Until Jarell signaled for me to come back there. I ran over. Jarell had taken Skylar out of the game, and they were standing by a fence a little way off. Skylar was staring at his cleats, face red, chest heaving as he tried to stifle sobs.

His dusty black canvas bat bag lay in the dirt like a dead dog.

"Come here, Skylar," Jarell said.

Sky kept his eyes on the ground and wouldn't budge.

"Over here. Right now. Are you afraid I'm gonna bite you?"

Sky shuddered. Tears sprang to my own eyes and I put my hand out to touch his shoulder, but Jarell waved at me to keep away. I obeyed him as diligently as I did in bed. It was like a dream where you can't move. What was wrong with me?

"Come on." There was a hard edge in Jarell's voice now. No wonder I obeyed this man; that edge was always there, I realized, just below the surface. Still, I was the adult. I should say something.

But Skylar stepped forward.

"I can't have anyone crying like that on my team, young man."

Skylar still wouldn't look up.

"Do you hear me? I can't have a crybaby on my team."

This was too much. Sky's gaze shot up. In the liberal, loving world of his life grown-ups didn't call kids names.

"Don't call him that," I said.

"Please stay out of this, Mom. Godmom. Whatever."

"Come on, Sky." I took his hand and handed him his bat bag.

"Crying does not have any purpose," Jarell said. "It

just shows your weakness to your enemy. And if you want to model tears and make, excuse me but, a lily-white mama's boy out of him, fine, it's your choice. But you both have some learning to do."

I certainly did. *Don't sleep with the love-of-your-life godson's baseball coach. Especially if he proves to be a Manticore. Cry it out. Cry as much as you fucking want.*

#6

I went on FU Cupid and found Carlton, a tall Canadian artist. Gave him four hearts. He hearted me back. We chatted and he e-mailed me a link to his website—large portraits that resembled religious medieval icons, made with tinted beeswax. Encaustic, it was called. He said they smelled like honey. That was enough for me to give him my number.

Carlton's voice was deep but somehow lilting. We decided to meet for coffee the next evening. Simple. Internet dating wasn't all that bad, I thought. And it was a good distraction from the dead girls now that Jarell was gone.

I met Carlton at Jack and the Bean. (When we were drinking, Bree and I used to joke that it was the wrong Jack, and we'd bring some of the right one to put in our coffee.) Carlton looked taller and thinner in person, dressed in a fawn-colored suede jacket, jeans, and heavy-soled brown leather shoes. He extended his hand to shake mine, quite formally, and we got iced coffee and sat outside on the sidewalk, breathing exhaust and watching the headlights of the cars curving away down the street.

He had a long face and a jagged nose, rather thin lips, but his eyes were pretty—round and hazel—if a bit myopic, behind his rectangular glasses.

"So how's this online thing been for you?" I said, not sure how else to start, since he hadn't yet.

"Strange. It hasn't worked out so far. One woman, she said I wasn't her type. But then we had so much in common and so she agreed to meet. She took one look at me and says, 'This isn't going to work for me,' and leaves."

"Oh, that's brutal. People are so brutal." I really felt for him. But maybe brutal was too strong a word. Brutal was what had happened to Michelle Babcock and the others. I almost brought it up but decided not to.

"How about you?" he asked.

"This is my first coffee date and so far it's working for me." His smile surprised me; it was warmer than I'd expected and erased thoughts of murder from my mind. "I like your paintings. I put a link to them on my blog."

"Thank you. I'd like to see it. Is there a theme?"

"Things that make life bearable. It's called *Love Monster.*"

"I'm flattered to be included. Why *monster*, though?"

"It started because my friend and I categorized men

we dated as different monsters. Ghouls, Manticores, Zombies . . ."

"What would I be?"

My turn to smile. I figured that even though he was an artist, his posture, his formality, and his full-time job qualified him as my very first Goblin. "But in a good way," I added when I told him.

"I think I'd prefer Vampire, even though they've been done to death, no pun intended."

"That, too. I'd say you're pretty elegant. And sexy." As I said it, I felt my clit stir. We just stared at each other for a moment and I wondered if he was hard.

"Well, if I painted you, you'd be a Madonna."

"Why's that?" I asked, thinking of the delicate portraits that smelled like honey. Once I'd read that some male artists imagined that they painted with their dicks.

"You have something very maternal about you. But also, if I may say so, quite sexy, too." His eyes moved over my body, down to my feet, in open-toed wedges, where his glance lingered.

My face warmed and I was instantly wet. We talked more about art and his work as an animator. LA, music, film. The subject matter wasn't too personal, but the tone was pure pillow talk.

We went for drinks at Bar Wire in the lobby of the White Hotel, which had been built in the twenties and even after its remodel in the nineties was rumored to be haunted. In the dark room lit by red chandeliers he had a glass of wine and I had cranberry and soda. Leaned against the suede of his jacket. Hard to imagine it as once a live thing, violently skinned. It was so pretty.

"I like your jacket." I felt drunk.

"I like your shoes." That should have been a clue.

As he drank the wine, he smiled more and more, slid the hem of my thrift shop chain-link-print silk wrap dress up my thigh. The veins in his hands were big, which signified a strong blood flow. Tingles scurried across the back of my legs.

"I haven't done this before with someone I've just met, and I hope you won't be offended, but I was wondering if you wanted to get a room."

There had been Jarell after Dash. Before Dash there had been others, more than was probably healthy for me. Every man I'd ever slept with, I had loved him in some way, found something to love about him. Not the men's strength as much as their vulnerability. Here was this one, rejected by some Internet bitch; he was a talented artist, soft-spoken, well dressed, articulate, sophisticated. "I haven't done this sober before, but yes."

The disconcertingly charming smile again. "Meaning, gotten a room with someone, or gotten a room with someone you don't know?"

"The latter."

"Are you sober? I mean, not just at the moment?"

I nodded.

"Yes? Cranberry and soda, eh? Good for you. I admire that discipline. How many years then?"

"Eleven."

"How about we round up to twelve and mess around half an hour for each year of your sobriety, Miss Catt? What do you say?"

We went across the street and bought condoms at the drugstore, giddy as teenagers. He paid for the room and I draped my scarf over the lamp to soften the light. His body was pale, pristine, lean, and yoga-toned. He knew how to place his cock in just the right spot. It made the tears spring to my eyes, and I worried that I'd scare him away. But he pulled out only to lick me, then slipped back in and fucked me just as I was still coming from the oral. He got up to use the bathroom and came back and showed me that he was hard again, standing next to the bed, sticking straight out. I rolled the condom on and we did it once more.

"I could go for hours," he said, and I thought of Jarell with a pang of longing that I was ashamed of. Not only because I missed him but because I was the one who had ultimately pushed him away. At least I wasn't thinking of Dash and the baby we would never have. *Don't think of Dash.* I gripped harder on to Carlton's lean torso and wept into his neck.

The next time we saw each other Carlton took me to a small, red-candle-lit restaurant in Venice. We sat in the window and ate white-bean hummus, spinach and baby shrimps on flatbread, and beet salad with feta cheese. When the waiter offered me wine, Carlton politely suggested pineapple-cucumber agua fresca. A dark-haired boy about Skylar's age stood in the window holding up hand-painted bangles and Carlton said, "I like his entrepreneurial spirit," and got up to go outside and buy me one. He slid it over my hand, and the weight of the bangle felt reassuring on my arm. It was painted with pink peonies on a red background, much like the dress I'd worn the night Dash left me.

I noticed that Carlton dropped his napkin three times during dinner and seemed to pause before he retrieved it. Once he said, "Lovely polish," about my toenails. "What's that color? Almost a pastel coral. It's really nice." He grinned.

I figured painters like colors, right?

After dinner we wandered down the street, past shops full of expensively distressed jeans and furniture, mosaics made from broken china and figurines, hedgehog-shaped teapots, orchids in birdcages, and tattooed and hennaed mannequins. Everything you needed to live in Los Angeles. I snapped photos for my blog; things looked magical to me again. There was even a new age bookstore that sold crystals and tarot cards. Carlton took my hand, pulled me inside, and asked the nose-ringed guy at the desk about the psychic reading they advertised.

When Nose Ring confirmed that, yes, a psychic was in, Carlton asked me if I'd like to try, and I agreed. What could it hurt? No one was going to predict an early death or anything. Yes, I really thought that.

We entered a small room where a woman with red hair sat at a table. "I don't use any cards," she said after we had introduced ourselves. "I go into a trance and speak to you about what I see. Sometimes I may make some odd sounds or gestures. Does that sound all right?"

We agreed. She seemed quite mild-mannered until she went "under." Then she glared and barked at us like a dog. Carlton cringed, pushed his glasses back on his nose, and crossed his legs.

"You, you, you," the woman said. "You are in pain. Yes, I sense such pain." *Bark bark.* "All will be well. Yes, all will be well. You were in another life. Together. In another life. Husband and wife." She turned her head toward Carlton but her eyes remained blank, as if she weren't really seeing him. "You were an artist. All will be well." To me: "You lived with his parents. In a cottage in the woods. You were angry at his mother. And she never accepted you." *Bark bark.*

What the fuck? I knew not to look at Carlton because we would giggle. Hysterically. Stomach crunchingly. I just knew.

"Many lives together. You two. But lots of pain. All will be well. You killed her."

I ventured to look at him and realized I was sitting

with my legs crossed in a position that mirrored his. He didn't turn his face to mine.

"But all will be well."

I slid the peony bangle up to my elbow and bit down hard on the inside of my mouth to keep from laughing. Nerves.

She turned her head directly to me and stared with those unseeing eyes. "All will be . . ." She stopped. She barked again. One hand went to her throat. She kept barking as if she couldn't stop. I bit the inside of my mouth harder and avoided Carlton's eyes. Finally the psychic was silent. She blinked at me. She said, "You will eventually learn to take care of yourself. To love yourself."

"Then will all be well?" Carlton asked. He winked at me.

The psychic shook her head. "No," she said. "Then you'll be on the other side."

We both burst out laughing; the tension was too much. The psychic stood up. She was out of her trance. I noticed creases in her face I hadn't seen before, and the way her makeup caked around her nostrils; she looked as if she'd aged about ten years. "We're finished now," she said.

Carlton and I ended up back at the hotel. I wondered why he hadn't suggested his place, but I didn't spend too much time worrying about that. I was trying to concentrate on what it would be like to have his big cock inside me and avoiding what the psychic had said afterward. *Then you'll be on the other side.* Dead.

Carlton undressed and lay on the bed watching me where I stood by the window that overlooked the streets below. I didn't have a scarf with me to soften the light. Maybe I should turn off the lamp? His cock was standing straight up again. "Take off your panties," he said.

I slipped them off from under my black satin, fifties-style dress, then started to unbutton it.

"No, leave the rest. Come sit over here, eh?" He took off his glasses; he meant sit on his face. I climbed up onto him, lifted the skirt of my dress, and eased my wetness down over his lips. He licked me gently, then harder, sucking softly on my clit as if it were dainty candy. I was worried my ass would suffocate him, but he seemed happy, stroking his cock in rhythm to my bounces.

"Now take out those big tits."

I unbuttoned my dress and undid my bra. He flipped me over so I was on my back and he stared at my breasts while he continued to touch himself. "Such nice big, soft titties," he said. Then he pushed up my skirt and slithered down so his mouth was on me again while he jammed his pelvis into the mattress. After I came, gasping for what felt like my last breath, tears sliding down my cheeks, he lay on his back and I lowered myself onto his legs and put him in my mouth.

"Do it sitting up. With your legs spread so I can see your pussy."

I did this, too.

Then he said, "May I please ask you to do something else?"

I waited. It was the first time he'd asked, although his commands had been spoken in the same rather refined tone, as if he were telling me to bring him iced tea.

"Can I put my toes in your pussy?"

I just felt confused, not even that shocked. It had seemed to come out of nowhere. I might have agreed.

But then he frowned. "My wife never lets me do that either."

Your what-the-fuck?

"She lives in Canada with her boyfriend but she visits me twice a year. We sort of sequester ourselves for that time and do yoga and meditate. She's deeply spiritual. If I'm seeing someone, they have to understand I won't be available at all for that time. It's just this thing we do. She's coming next week, actually."

"I'm not feeling so great." I skittered away from him, clutching my belly, suddenly aware of the way the flesh rolled there. The queasiness congealing in my gut was as much about me as him. Why had I done this? "I need to go now."

He eyed me coldly and put his glasses back on. "Okay, I was just being honest. I'm sorry if that bothers you. She's my soul mate and she left me for another man. Do you know what that's like?" Behind the coldness I recognized raw hurt.

"Actually, I do," I said, pulling on my clothes, sucking in my belly to tug up the zipper on the side of my dress. Adding to the humiliation, it caught my flesh with tiny metal teeth. Maybe he would tell me to stay. I might have stayed.

"She says she still loves me but she's not attracted to me. It's very painful."

"I'm sorry," I said. "Really. I have to go."

He stood up, naked, facing me. He was still hard. "Why are you upset? Because I have a young, thin wife who's a yoga teacher? Because I see her twice a year?" His voice was louder now, almost, maybe, somewhat desperate. "It's not like you're in love with me or anything. Are you? You're not in love with me or something, so why should you care?"

I shouldn't have cared. I just wanted to let him fuck me again. But he was obviously in love with his young, hot, spiritual yoga-teacher wife; I couldn't even pick up my meditation beads anymore. And that crazy psychic said that Carlton had killed me in another life.

I stumbled to the door, holding my shoes. "It's okay. Sorry. Thanks. Thank you. I'll get a cab home."

The hall smelled of air coolant and fried food. The red-and-gold carpet scratched under my feet. Ghosts wept in the mirrors.

After I got home and went to bed, I dreamed Carlton and I were walking around in a dark cavernous store filled with china and glass figurines of women that kept shattering into shards in my hands. The store seemed to go on forever. Finally we found a door. Inside there was a dark room with pedestals everywhere. On each one were red-veined white marble statues of naked female body parts. Feet, legs, torsos, breasts, heads.

Then I was one of them—just my head and nude, limbless torso balanced on a pedestal.

In the morning, I called Shana and told her about Carlton.

"You didn't drink, did you?"

"No, we were at Bar Wire and he was, but I wasn't tempted even. But why did I sleep with him? He could have been anybody. He could have been the Hollywood Killer." (In spite of what the psychic had said, I was sure this wasn't true.) "I make myself sick." (This was true.)

"You need to call me and Bree every day," she said. "And a minimum of three meetings a week. I've been way too easy on you."

After the meeting Shana had to leave so I went to fellowship at Planet Pie alone, and the writer guy from the other day was there. He came over to my table and introduced himself. Dean Berringer.

His handshake was firm and his brown eyes crinkled at the edges when he smiled. "I appreciated your share the other day, Catt," he said. Five o'clock shadow, bushy eyebrows, a male smell. I missed that—burrowing into Dash's armpit. A place to forget the world. "Sounds like you've been through a lot."

"What about you?" I asked.

"Nothing too dramatic. I'd been sitting at my desk for way too long, stuck on this part of my book, and I knew I had to be with my people."

"You're a writer?" Feigning ignorance.

"Yeah, if you can call it that. In this town you're not really unless it says *screen* in front of it."

"In some places it has to say *of actual book* after," I said.

"Yeah, but they don't acknowledge me in New York. So Cal surrealism. Indie press. Postpunk LA."

"Still," I said.

"And you?"

"I just cut hair."

He removed his hat to reveal a receding hairline, not like Cyan's and Dash's but getting there at a slower pace. "Can you do anything with this?"

"Leopard spots. Tiger stripes. Zebra."

He put his hat back on. "I was thinking more along the lines of a magical potion to make it grow back."

"It looks sexy on you," I said. "I like bald men. High testosterone or something, right?" I was out of breath

again like in the meeting, sweating through my tur-
quoise nylon blouse.

"I'd like to take you out after a meeting sometime."

I bought his first novel at Bookgarten, the only remaining local indie bookstore (they also sold garden sup-
plies in order to make ends meet). *The Eurydices* was
about a sculptor named Owen Orr whose wife dies of a
brain tumor. Grief stricken, he becomes involved with
his models, all of whom resemble his wife in some way.
One of the women accuses him of raping her. All the
women are part of a cult and they tear him to pieces in
the end.

The book was well written and with its shock value
made me forget everything else. Bree was always surprised that I could watch and read the scariest things,
even alone by myself at night. I needed the book and
movie monsters to chase away the ghosts in my head.

Dean Berringer wore a faded pink T-shirt with a skull
on it. The skull had black roses for eyes. The whole
thing, even the pink and the roses, only added to his
masculine look. I thought, *Uh-oh.*

"My name's Dean and I'm an alcoholic."

"Hi, Dean."

"The reason I'm sharing today is that I've been kind

of disturbed by something." He frowned and rubbed his forehead. "I'm a writer and the book I've been working on is similar to what's going on in the news, with that Hollywood Serial Killer thing. I realize this is just coincidence, but it is really upsetting to me; I can't stop thinking about it. The guy in my book kills women and cuts off their body parts to construct a female zombie. Like these women they keep finding. I mean, the body parts. I mean, I write horror, I've been writing it for years, but nothing like this has ever happened. I guess it would be worse if I wrote and published the book first, but I don't know. Like it was some copycat killing that I started. Anyway, thank you for letting me share."

Even as I tried to suppress a shudder, I knew I wouldn't skip the coffee date we'd made. If anything, I wanted to talk to him more. As if he might have some insight into what was haunting all of us.

"So I appreciated your share," I said when we were seated at Jack and the Bean.

He nodded and ran his thumb around the rim of his coffee cup. "Thank you. I wasn't sure I should say anything."

"That's kind of the deal, I guess. I mean, so they tell me."

"So they do. But I'm glad you decided to have coffee with me anyway."

We sat looking at each other, without speaking for a

moment. Then he said, "I just wish I understood the relationship between my book and that freak out there."

"Collective unconscious, maybe? You picked up on something, I guess. I liked your first book, though. I'm going to write it up for my blog."

"It's pretty dark. Although I suppose after my share you would know that about me anyway."

"Dark can be good." I squinted at him, the sun light hitting my eye line as the sun edged lower in the sky. "It helps me forget my own shit."

"I wouldn't guess you'd feel that way. From looking at you."

I asked him why and he touched the sleeve of the gauze blouse I'd borrowed from Bree. "Flowers everywhere."

I shrugged. "It's my friend's. She made it. And flowers can be dark."

His eyebrows went up. "Really?"

"Yes. Poisonous ones. Psychotropic ones. Carnivorous."

"Right. Well spoken."

"I did my senior thesis at UCLA on death in Los Angeles literature and music," I said.

"Very impressive. Didion, West, Chandler, the Doors?"

"Exactly. And also Eve Babitz, Steve Erickson, Janet Fitch, Bret Easton Ellis, X, Tupac."

"To Live and Die in L.A."

"That's the one."

"Mmmm. So the flower is darker than I thought."

"I was goth in high school," I said, fake-scowling at him. "Don't mess with me."

"Duly noted. Which school?"

"Fairfax High."

"You're a local. More creds for your thesis."

He was from upstate New York, had gone to Harvard, lived in Boston, came here when someone optioned one of his books for the screen. He'd gone through a bad divorce after his professor wife had an affair with one of her grad students.

"Fifteen years younger than her. They just had their first kid."

That was his wound, and I realized those bloody rips were the things that made me fall in love with someone more than poetry or music or strength or beauty ever could.

"Tell me, if you don't mind, it might be too personal. But what you are trying to forget?" he asked me. "Something to do with your share at the meeting?"

"It's a longish story."

"I have all night."

It was if we were touching—our conversation had that kind of energy, a rush back and forth between us.

We stood at the curb. I'd walked to the café but Dean had a red Triumph and he asked if I wanted a ride home. I put on the helmet; he fastened it under my chin. I slung my leg over the seat, pressed against his rippling back. Hot skin beneath the T-shirt, broad chest; my legs clung to his hips. Books and bikes; we really might as well be fucking already.

He was going too fast. The wind whipped against my face burning my lips and cheeks. I bent my head down behind his shoulder. My eyes stung. We ripped the air, we tore it up like silk. I thought, *Fuck you, Dash. Look at me now, you asshole. Check me out, Jarell. Carlton, you fucking toe-sucker.*

Dean held my hand as we walked up the stairs to the bungalow. He kissed me soft on the mouth and then we were entwined and then his hand was on my ass and his pelvis was against mine and I didn't have to wonder about his cock.

"I should go," he said. Then, more softly: "Should I?"

I shook my head, thinking of the dark in my home. The Dash-less dark. The bumps in the night. The Hollywood Serial Killer harvesting lithe limbs of his victims. How they were alone when he got them, no daddies or husbands or boyfriends to protect them. *That's why boyfriends are a good idea.* Dean Berringer might write horror but I doubted he was dangerous in any way. "Come in."

I opened the door and we stumbled into the living room as if we were still drunks. Sasha darted away into the shadows like a phantom cat. I led Dean to the couch, where we fell on top of each other, kissing, kissing, kissing. Soft lips, strong teeth, a tongue somewhere in between the pressure of the two. Dean's fingers slid down between my legs pushing into me; I bucked up against them. I had tears in my eyes from excitement, and mild fear, not sorrow, not love, I told myself, like the tears I used to get as a child listening to scary stories at slumber parties, and I blinked them back so I could see him better in the dark. His eyes glittered black with light from the streetlamp. He had lines in his face, was probably nearing fifty. I found myself wondering if he wanted children. I would have let him fuck me without a condom if he'd asked. But in my bedroom he took one out and dutifully put it on. I hated the rubber between us; I wanted to feel him come into me. He spread my legs and put himself inside, pushed his pelvis so that he couldn't go any farther. More tears came to my eyes. It hurt a little. I wanted that hurt, wanted to erase the debacle with Carlton. Wanted to erase my five years of marriage with each thrust. And Jarell, too. Maybe, weirdly, especially Jarell. We'd only been together a few times, I reminded myself. It had been only about the sex. And I had ended it. In my head there had been potential, but only in my head. Was this thing with Dean something more?

Dean said, "If you were mine, I'd buy you a 1920s mansion, with hundreds of white roses in front, and a huge library with leatherbound books from floor to ceiling, ladders to reach them all, and a big, tiled pool that was always warm, like a bathtub, surrounded by statues of naked nymphs, and eucalyptus trees. You could open your own salon and we'd go to restaurants and movies every night and you could review them on your blog. We'd have lavish parties every weekend and travel to Europe and I'd buy you black lingerie and vintage dresses and give you as many babies as you wanted." At this last, I came so hard I thought I would never come back. It seemed he already knew me so well. Or maybe he just knew women well.

We lay together for a while, my head on his chest, his hands in my hair, making me purr. He asked me about my childhood and we discovered the things we shared growing up—alcoholic mothers who had died of cancer, abandoning fathers, screaming fights, and sexual betrayals. The usual. He was even more my type than I had realized, our pain-pillow-talk more of an aphrodisiac than sex; I wanted him to fuck me again. But he seemed tired.

My favorite music mix was playing. Nic Cave, PJ Harvey, Björk, Tori Amos. Portals to other worlds. I hadn't been able to play it since Dash left. How pathetic that I could only listen to my favorite music if a man was there. *But you are listening,* I told myself. *And, yes, he is still here. Be glad of that.*

"May I stay?"

In answer I kissed his stubbled cheek. But I couldn't sleep with him there so I lay beside him, forgetting how I ever breathed without thinking about it. At about 3:00 a.m. I finally fell . . .

I'd forgotten to close the curtains so the brutal sun woke us whitely. I got up before him, to brush my teeth, and checked my reflection; I looked like shit.

When I went back to bed, hoping for a morning fuck to substitute for sleep, he said he had a seriously bad headache. I gave him an Advil, made coffee, and then he kissed me quick and left. Taking with him my heart, like a small, viscous purse.

I struggled through work with cut-glass corneas; I was getting too old for late-night sex with relative strangers. When I got home, I wanted to e-mail Skylar but I worried I'd upset him; he was such a little empath. So I told myself he'd reach out if he needed me—then I would answer him of course. The only new e-mails I had were from FU Cupid: "The lines around your eyes are scary clear signs of aging or drug use yet still you play hard to get. LOVE."

Had I corresponded with this person? I looked at the picture. The man was in his early fifties, pasty white, balding, with a sagging face and goggle eyes. In one of the photos he had his arm around a girl. The caption read, "With my ex. She was way younger than me. Big tits, no waist, no ass, great lay." Another picture showed him gripping a mic and wearing a studded belt under his belly paunch. The caption read, "I'm a F-ing rock star." Under interests he'd listed, "Hot chicks, Sex, Mass Murderers, Cults, Manson, Dahmer, Ramirez, the Hollywood Serial Killer." I should have been able to delete the message and block the guy from my account, but I just sat there staring at the computer until black spots swam around my eyes like drowned flies.

In a month I had slept with three men I didn't really know, while my neighbor—Michelle Babcock was her name—was slaughtered and cut into pieces.

Already, by then, something intricate and vital was falling apart inside of me.

I waited to hear from Dean. He had said, "If you were mine . . ." Was I that naïve that I bought it? No, but I chose to anyway. Especially in light of Michelle Babcock's death.

I went to meetings, but mostly because I was hoping to see Dean there. I called Shana every day as promised and talked about Dash and Jarell and Michelle Babcock, but managed to avoid the subject of my new obsession.

Bree wasn't going out as much—there were problems with Dr. Vampire, and after Michelle Babcock's death she didn't feel like partying, she said—so I didn't get to have Skylar or take him to his games. Which was probably for the best considering what was going on with me. Fortunately he called me a few nights a week and sometimes came in to the salon to do his homework after school. This was always the light of my day, but the fact that it didn't pull me entirely out of my depression pointed to the darkening of my mind.

When I was with Bree and Skylar, no one talked about Jarell. I knew Bree had met him when she went to tell him not to call her son names (he had apologized) and was just being thoughtful by not mentioning him after that. He had probably hit on her already.

I didn't go to the gym. I should have, I should have checked up on Scott, brought him food, seen how his new apartment was. But I was afraid of a long conversation that would reveal what I'd been up to, so I only texted him a few quick words. He replied in kind.

The only person who checked up on me regularly at that time, besides Skylar, was Cyan. He had been sending me pictures for *Love Monster* and little texts now and then, but he also called the day after Michelle Babcock's photo was on the news when he realized she had lived in my neighborhood. I told him I hadn't seen anything suspicious and that she hadn't died at home so I wasn't any more nervous about where I lived than I'd been before. And I had the alarm system, thanks to him. He made me promise to stay in touch, especially if anything seemed strange.

Alone in my apartment with Sasha and the TV and my cell phone, I stared into the mirror at the lines around my eyes, thought about the Hollywood Serial Killer, and waited for Dean's call. I was aware I had transferred my desperation about Dash and Darcy London, and about the murders, to Dean, but it didn't lessen the urgency of the feeling, as if toads were in my belly, trying to leap out of my throat and infest the rooms.

Dean texted me that his publisher had added a few cities to his book tour and he'd be in touch; weeks passed and he never called. I thought of trying him back but decided against it. Jarell was gone. Dash had left one message checking on me when he'd heard about Michelle Babcock, but my husband was very gone.

It was Cyan who returned.

#7

When Cyan came to my door (this time he had checked first to see if it was okay), he looked tan and unshaven and was wearing shorts, a T-shirt, and flip-flops, not his usual plaid-flannel-lined Seattle hoodie. I'd just gotten home from work and my skin felt sticky with hairspray from the day. I'd had nonstop clients who all needed a little extra TLC and I was pretty drained. Serina, who had three children and an awesome husband, cried while I gave her a Brazilian blowout; she'd just had a miscarriage. Lisa-Anne was pregnant and complaining about the exuberant thickness and length of her hormone-enhanced hair. Karli was getting married and needed her extensions redone but hadn't yet told her fiancé that her locks weren't real. Deirdre, the model, couldn't get any work because her agency said she was too thin. She weighed about ninety pounds; her lips and eyes looked bigger and more voluptuous than ever in contrast with her bony jaw and sunken cheeks. When I offered her the name of a sliding-scale clinic that specialized in eating disorders and suggested a 12-step program, I saw her eyes glaze over. So I gave her a discount on her bob (her long hair was falling out) and an extralong hug and told her to call me if she needed anything.

We were all really just freaked out by the murders, especially Michelle's, because of how close she'd lived to the salon, but none of us talked about it. By the time I got home I needed some strong, male energy.

It was evening and Cyan and I sat on the balcony watching the evening sky pinken the atmosphere, listening to the sounds of traffic and sipping Perrier. The air smelled of charcoal fluid, flames, and meat. I felt as if Cyan had woken me from a long, complicated dream that I wanted to get back to. Even the most complex and terrifying dreams were easier to handle than my life, it seemed.

Later I made pasta with pesto, which we ate in the kitchen, though I mostly just picked at my food. He asked me about my new alarm system and if there had been any other sounds in the night.

I told him no.

"To be honest, I've been kind of obsessing over that thing happening to someone who lived so close to you. Anyone you see on a regular basis that makes you uncomfortable?"

"Besides the guys I meet at work and online?" I tried to joke.

"Seriously, Catt." He said he had gone to Body Farm

that morning after he left me and that a strange "stretch-face" dude was there, training some women.

"Big Bob," I told him.

"That's his name? Big Bob? What's his story?"

"Bodybuilder, steroid freak, creepy but harmless," I said.

"Okay, if you say so. Anyone else?"

I ended up telling him what had happened with Stu, F-ing rock star, and Dean. I avoided talking about Jarell or Carlton.

"If I can speak frankly . . ."

I nodded.

"You need to take better care of yourself, Catt. What's all this about?"

I shrugged, not wanting to look at him.

"Tell me."

"I try so hard," I said. "Everything I do, I keep trying and trying to be better. To be good enough. But it's not enough." Even as I spoke the words, I was ashamed of them. I sounded petulant and weak.

"There's no such thing as perfection."

I flicked my eyes at him sideways. He was frowning, thinking.

"What?" I said.

"As a kid I had a dog, a puppy, Bella. The most gorgeous dog, smart, sweet. I mean, this was the best dog in the world. Perfect. But she died while I was giving her a bath with a hose in the yard. Heart defect. There is no perfection."

The puppy in the photograph. Dash hadn't wanted to talk about her when I had asked. "I'm sorry. That must have been so hard for you when you were a kid."

"Much worse happens to children. But my point is, you are a smart, beautiful, sweet woman. With an artist's eye and hand. And you have a beautiful, strong heart, Catt. Any man should be able to see that."

Warmth spread through my body, unbidden. I didn't want these words to be coming from Cyan's mouth. Why couldn't Dash have said them? Or, better yet, someone new, who wasn't his brother? At the same time, I needed these words. Like food. Like water. Like sex.

"If they can't, it's better to be alone, trust me," he said. I frowned. Why hadn't I learned that lesson? He must have interpreted my look as disappointment rather than regret because he added, "You're the one who calls it a monster."

Love monster. In my blog. "What about you?"

"What about me?"

"Is it better to be with someone or alone?"

He smiled—a rare occurrence—the hard angles of his face gentling, eyes brightening as he glanced up at me from under sensually heavy eyelids. "Why do you ask?"

Maybe I was trying to distance myself from him. Maybe I was trying to bring him closer. Maybe I was just expressing my concern for someone I cared about. "I asked Dash when I first met you if you had a girlfriend, and he said why, when you could spend time with all those models."

Cyan shook his head. "That sounds like something he would say. But you didn't really answer my question."

"What was your question again?"

"Why do you ask me if it's better to be alone? For me."

"I'm just curious. You seem content to be by yourself. But I wonder if anyone really is."

He smoothed a hand over his sculptural head. "Like I said, being alone is better than being with the wrong person, that's all I'm sure of."

"Have you ever found the right person?"

He gazed away, into the darkness, musing. "I don't know. I've found parts of her in different people, I guess."

There was an awkward silence.

"May I take your photograph?"

It startled me, as if he'd suggested something much more intimate. When I realized he hadn't, I thought of those deer women with wet hair and asked him, "Why?"

"Let's see. I'm a photographer. I take portraits of people. You're very lovely. How's that?"

In the shot I like best, the woman who is me is sitting on my unmade mattress with Sasha curled up in a ball behind her; the woman's arms are wrapped around her torso and she's looking away from the camera. Her hair, in a small, wispy ponytail, is very black, her skin so white, her eyes like worlds.

Cyan came over, knelt beside the bed, and showed it to me.

"How come you're so good?" I said. "I usually hate pictures of myself."

"It's all in the subject matter."

"Why are you being this way?" I blinked back tears but one rogue escaped.

Cyan lifted his lens and shot me like that, the tear glistening on my cheek. "Sorry," he said. "I'm sorry. I shouldn't have taken that one but I couldn't resist." He reached in his back pocket and handed me a tissue from a small pack.

I dabbed at my eyes, blackening the tissue with mascara and eyeliner. "You never answered my question?"

"What question?"

"Why are you being . . ."

"Being what?"

"So kind."

"I have no agenda, Catt. I hope you know I would never . . ."

I leaned forward, leaned into him, closed my eyes. He reached out to keep me from falling, caught me. I thought of a Pina Bausch dance performance I had once seen and posted, of a man and woman walking across a concrete plaza; she kept dropping like a plank into his arms. You thought she was going to crack her skull but he caught her. Every time he caught her.

With one arm around my shoulders Cyan took his other hand and pressed it to my heart, exactly where that organ beat, as if he could see it through my skin and flesh. He grasped the back of my neck and pulled me to him and our mouths brushed, just brushed, just enough for me to feel the dry skin on his lips. Then we crashed into a world-obliterating kiss.

When we separated simultaneously, there was something in his eyes I couldn't understand. Surprise? Tenderness? Sorrow? Pain? Maybe even aversion. I wasn't sure. But I knew this—my vital organs were sinking stones.

I closed my eyes so as not to see his expression anymore. All I wanted was pleasure, a way to kill the hurt. His lips felt as soft and full as they looked, soothing me as I suckled them. His hands were back on my neck, on my shoulders, gently tugging at my bra, touching my breasts, flirting with the nipples through the thin fabric of my blouse. He laid me down on the mattress, still kissing me. I moaned as he cupped my whole left breast in one hand, holding my heart. I could have come just from that touch.

I felt him undoing my blouse, button by button, taking off my skirt, unhooking my bra, sliding my panties over my hips. Everything gentle and slow and so easy. I opened my eyes and saw him standing above me, looking down at my face, not at my breasts, not between my legs. His eyes had softened again.

"You're so different from other women," he told me.

I froze and put my hands over my belly. I wasn't like those girls he photographed. Is that what he meant?

He seemed to know what I was thinking because he brushed my hair away from my forehead with the tips of his fingers. "You're loving. You have depth."

Dash didn't want me but Cyan did. For him, I was enough. "Please," I whispered. "Cyan. Please." I grabbed him by the back of his neck and pulled his mouth to mine.

"Is it okay? Are you sure?"

"Yes," I said. I was sure.

Then Cyan unzipped himself and pushed inside of me with one tight thrust, and I had exactly what I wanted. The little death. But it was a big death, really, the most wrenching orgasm of my life.

The room had darkened completely, purple orchid pollen clinging to our skins, stamens lapping at us like tongues. We rolled into the night flowers together. I lay with my head on his chest, listening to the grainy sound of his heartbeat, my hands reaching up to feel the shape of his jaw, down to palpate the breadth of his torso, his narrow hip bones. We might have stayed there forever. But he got up, gathered his clothes, and went into the bathroom. When he came back fully dressed, he sat on the edge of the bed with his head in his hands.

"I'm sorry, Catt," Cyan said, without look at me. "I didn't plan that. I guess I've been wishing it would happen in some ways, but I would never . . . I'm so sorry. I never want to hurt you."

What had happened? What had we done? I had

blamed Dash for being a sex addict. I was the worst addict of all.

Cyan stood up. "I'll let myself out. I have to get back to Seattle, anyway. That's what I came to tell you. I just wanted to tell you to take care of yourself and let you know I was leaving."

No.

#8

The next night, after working late, I went to Body Farm to try to sweat out as much of the past few days as possible. Big Bob was there, of course, training Leila, who wore her hair in two braids. This made her look younger and seemed to emphasize the tiny spray of freckles on her nose. She smiled, and I felt the same way I did in high school if a popular girl acknowledged me, the way I used to feel when Bree first became my friend. Proud but also anxious that if I became too close, she might take everything I had. And now that was Cyan, too. *But you don't have Cyan.* Bob's mouth remained grim as he gestured for Leila to continue pumping iron.

"Where's Scott?" I asked.

"Not feeling well," Bob sneered, a vein in his neck bulging. "Stayed home again."

I'd texted Scotty—no answer. I did a short, distracted workout. Leila, fresh from the shower, her hair still wet, waved good-bye to me as she left.

It was getting dark outside and the gym was weirdly empty. The air was on too high and my skin goose-bumped.

While I was finishing up on the StairMaster, I saw, in the mirror, Bob staring fixedly at my butt and rubbing his chin. I turned around and glared at him.

"Looking good there, Catt. I'd like an ass like that," he said. And grinned.

On the way home I stopped at the market and went by Scott's house. He answered, disheveled and unshaven; usually his skin was as soft and smooth as Skylar's.

"Where've you been?" I asked with more edge to my voice than I'd intended. As if it were somehow his fault that I'd slept with Cyan.

"Here. Sorry I didn't answer you. I haven't been feeling great. Stomach flu or something."

I made him soup with the miso I'd bought for him earlier and sat with him on his futon while he ate it.

"Poor baby," I said, feeling his forehead with the back of my hand. "Don't not answer my texts anymore, though, even if you're dying."

He laughed weakly and his eyes peered up at me through his lenses, asking what was going on.

I couldn't tell Scott about Dean. I didn't want to upset him by talking about what Stu had said to me or about Michelle Babcock. I especially didn't feel I could talk about Cyan. Maybe if I had confided in Scott, he would have been able to tell me more about what was really happening with him. But instead of asking how he was in any meaningful way, I asked if he thought Big Bob was acting extra-weird.

"Of course, he's always been weird."

"But now especially, right?"

Scott frowned at me. "Where are you going with this?"

"Oh God," I said. "I don't know. Now I feel like a complete asshole."

"No, no, Catt." Scott shook his head back and forth, so his hair, which he'd let get longer than usual, fell across his face. "I just think you're under a lot of stress right now. With Dash and everything. And maybe you're feeling a little extra-sensitive to things."

"Yeah," I said. "Sure, I'm sure that's all it is."

"Catt?"

"I'm sorry. I didn't mean to freak out. I know you have a lot going on, too. Have you talked to Emi?" At least I asked him that.

"No, she won't speak to me. Thank God I have you, though."

"Do you need to see a doctor?" I said. "I'll go with you." Scott hated doctor's appointments.

"No, no, I'm good. Just been a little run-down."

When I left his place, I thought I was doing okay, but by the time I got to my neighborhood I was a wreck. Hungry, Angry, Lonely, Tired. I hadn't eaten all day, I hadn't slept well, I'd just spent an hour with Scott but it was like neither of us were really there. And angry, I was angry. At almost everyone and everything in my life. At Dash and Darcy London. At Jarell and Dean and Carlton. At Bree for suggesting I sign up for FU Cupid. At the women at work for draining me with their needs. At myself, most of all. *You slept with Cyan. You slept with Cyan.* The corner liquor store flashed its neon sign at me. The posters of phallic bottles and cleavage. Tatted flesh, because of the neighborhood we were in. It would be so easy to buy a bottle of Jack, take him home, and finish him off. . . .

Instead, I picked my original addiction—Dash.

I called him. It was the first time I'd called since he'd moved out, although I'd been tempted, especially after the message he'd left about Michelle Babcock. As I punched the buttons, I realized how amazing it was that I'd resisted calling him this long, especially since he had reached out first after what happened to our neighbor. But my discipline was blown now. He answered.

"I almost had a drink," I said by way of a greeting. *I fucked your brother.*

"Catt?"

"No, it's your mom," I said. Which was a shitty thing to say. First because she was dead, and second because he hated anyone to even mention her. "I'm sorry."

He ignored my shitty-ness and my apology. "When you say almost, how close was it?"

"I drove past the liquor store. And thought about stopping." I realized how stupid I sounded.

"Listen, Catt, I can't really talk right now, I'm in the middle of something, but I hear that you need help." His vocal cords sounded strained, the way he did for a week after a gig. "Do you still feel safe in that neighborhood? After . . ."

"I got an alarm system," I said flatly.

"Have you called Bree and Shana tonight?" Dash asked.

"Not yet."

"Can you do that now?"

"Yes."

"Okay, good. Because I can't talk right now. But you can call me if you can't reach them. When's the last time you went to a meeting?"

"A few days ago."

"Okay, so you need to get to one as soon as possible. Are you meditating?"

It was almost funny. Meditating? Really? I didn't answer.

"But call Shana now, okay? Right now?"

I was silent, gulping down a sudden, errant sob.

"Catt? I care about you. I didn't mean to hurt you like that. I hope someday we—"

I hung up.

I didn't go to the liquor store.

I called Shana, who left the charity fund-raiser she

was attending with her girlfriend, Gia, and came right away, dressed in a narrow, white tuxedo-style suit and hot-pink satin Manolos. For someone so pretty and delicate looking, she was one tough bitch when she wanted to be.

"You have to do the steps again, Catt. I'm not going to waste my time with you otherwise," she chastised.

I nodded, eyes on the floor.

"Honesty, open-mindedness, and doing the right thing. It's our mantra. All of us. Remember that."

"Okay, I will, I just . . ."

"You just what?"

I didn't want to do all the steps again. Especially the Fourth Step inventory. Especially now. I would list Dash, Darcy London, Jarell, Carlton, Dean, Stu, Big Bob, the psycho on FU Cupid, Cyan, my mother, my father. Bree for suggesting I go online to find a man. Even Shana for guilt-tripping me about my behavior. I felt they had harmed and threatened my *self-esteem, emotional security* and *sexual relations,* if I used the AA terms. What could I have done differently? Not married a sex addict, not had sex with men who didn't love me in order to relieve the pain of my life, avoided Stu and told him to come back when Bree was there, joined a different gym so I wouldn't have to see Big Bob, not gone online to find a man so soon after Dash left, not let Cyan get so close to me, *not slept with Cyan,* gone to more meetings, called Shana more often. What about my mother and my father? I didn't have the same choice there. *You were just a little kid. You didn't ask to be born to them, to have to witness the fighting, the betrayals, the abandonment.* But I could have responded to my father when he tried to contact me, I could have sought out my mother and held her hand when she died. There, I'd done my inventory. I didn't need to write it down or think about it anymore. Still, I promised Shana I would hit a meeting in the morning and go every night after work for the whole week.

#9

Spring moved into summer like a child resentfully becoming an adolescent, mortified by sweat glands, acne,
and pubic hair. The excessive heat we'd had in April
got worse and set everyone on edge. The air smelled
flammable, gasoline prices and unemployment jumped
again, fires still raged through the canyons, murder
rates went up. At Body Farm I switched back and forth
between the news (explosions, fires, floods, tornadoes,
rapes, shootings) and, when it got too depressing, reality shows, which sometimes made me equally de-
pressed, if in a very different and ludicrous way. On
one dating show a woman was considered crazy for
"stalking" the men she dated by googling them before-
hand. I pleaded guilty to this behavior. On another
show celebrities compared the scent of their vaginas as
if this were sanctioned public behavior. Not guilty. Anorexic models were told they had no personality to speak

of and thrown, hobbling and sobbing, out of the competition. Thin women with minuscule noses, shoulder pads, and high heels bitched out the fatties, threw away their clothes, and made them cry. On an entertainment-gossip show a famous actress had her breasts and womb removed to prevent the cancers that had killed her mother. Darcy London was featured with her baby, Python. She'd started a line of punk-rock baby clothes, called Mommy's Lil' Punk, complete with pink and blue skeleton-shaped safety pins holding them together. The biggest local news story was still the Hollywood Serial Killer.

I read about the murders constantly now, staring at pictures of Mandy, Adrienne, and Michelle, trying to understand what might have happened to them.

I didn't leave the house much, except for work, errands, and meetings, which I'd limited to three a week, telling a displeased Shana that was all I could manage and that I hadn't been tempted to drink since the day after Cyan left anyway (which wasn't entirely true; I'm sorry, Shana). Another untruth—okay lie—was to Scott about a pinched nerve in my neck that was acting up, so I could avoid Body Farm. The thought of going there and seeing Big Bob's dry-tanned taxidermy face made me sweat and set my heart pounding, so much that I didn't need to work out.

#

One night I was home watching TV in the living room. I dug my hands into the secret recesses and crevices of the couch, absentmindedly looking for lost change or pens. My fingers felt something hard and I pulled at it. A piece of chain? I pulled some more and released a delicate golden necklace with a word written in cursive script that reminded me of the pleasant dreaminess of a 1970s folk-rock album cover.

California, it said. I had no idea to whom it belonged. Maybe Bree—it looked like her style. She picked up when I called her.

I realized, when I heard her voice in the night, that maybe I had been pulling away from her. Only seeing her at work where we were too busy to really talk. It seemed she had been pulling away from me, too. Ever since, what? Dash's leaving? (Was she worried I'd be too much to handle without him?) Cyan's asking me to dinner? (Was she jealous? No way.) When I told her that I was tempted to take a drink? Did that make her worry about her own sobriety? Or was I imagining her distance, projecting? There were too many layers.

"Did you lose a necklace? It says *California*?"

"No, why?"

"I just found it in my couch."

"Not mine. How are you doing, anyway? Are you okay?"

"Sure," I said not too convincingly. "I haven't felt like going out much. But I miss you and Sky."

"Do you want to take him to the gym this Sunday? Maybe have him overnight?"

"Do you have a date?"

"No, I broke up with the Vampire." In all this time we still called him that, which had never boded well for him, I guess.

"Well then, don't you want Skylar with you?"

"Yes, but he keeps asking about you."

"Why Body Farm? Doesn't he want to go to the park or something?"

"He wants to start weight training to help with baseball. His coach says—"

"Jarell?" My own voice saying his name startled me. Bree was the one taking Skylar to practice now. I assumed Jarell had hit on her. *Resentment.* But I knew that was wrong. It wasn't Bree's fault that men desired her. I'd had my chance with him.

"Yes, he suggested it. And I thought it would be good for both of you to see Scott on a Sunday. Especially when Bob's not around."

I'd told her about the ass comment, which made her hate Big Bob more than she already did. But her membership was practically free and he let her bring Skylar, so she still went.

"And to work out?" I said. *She thinks I'm getting fat.*

"Catt, stop, you're being impossible."

I was. I was being impossible. All this had started because I'd slept with Cyan. Which was the fault of

F-ing Rock Star. Who only messaged me because Bree told me to go online. Which I did because Dean didn't call me back. I only slept with him because Dash left me. *You could have decided not to marry a sex addict.*

"I'm sorry. I'd love to take Sky," I said. "Thank you for asking me."

When he was born, I was the one who held him first. I never said it to Bree, but I didn't want to let go of him when I laid him on her belly. She had trouble nursing and I helped him latch onto her. I stayed in her room all night, holding him while she slept, waking her when he needed milk. The nurse came in the morning while Bree was in the restroom and saw me sitting there, staring down at him in my arms; he was translucent as an angel.

"Seems like you kind of like him, huh?" the nurse said, winking, mistaking me for the mom. "You think you're going to keep him?"

He was the one person I needed to see more than any other, the one person who made me remember why I was alive in the first place, why life mattered at all. I hadn't seen him enough. Yes, Bree'd had him more, but I was also afraid to expose him to what was going on inside of me. *Suck it up, Catt. Get it together.*

The gym was quiet when Skylar and I got there on Sunday. Since it was Big Bob's day off, the whole place had a more relaxed feel. The music was softer and the air-conditioning wasn't blasting. Sky and I got on the treadmills side by side. When he was about six, he'd been watching cartoons and sped the machine up too fast. Scott was all the way across the room but somehow managed to catch him, practically in midair. That was how I'd met Scott. I'd told him he was a hero and he blushed. I mean, what grown men actually blush? Scott and Sky were friends from that day on, always talking sports and Harry Potter and Scott taught Skylar how to shake hands—"Firm, all the way from the shoulder"; Sky was very proud to have accomplished this, and I felt bad that no one else had taught him before. Soon Bree and I loved Scott, too.

He came over to Skylar and me, that Sunday in June, feet planted, wearing his usual nylon sweatpants.

"Nice to see you, Catt." He sounded so formal and even his hug was a little stiff. Turning to Sky: "What's up, buddy?"

Skylar shrugged and did that thing where he tries not to smile and show all his teeth. Scott messed up his hair. "Go, Dodgers." They high-fived.

"How are you?" I asked. "I'm sorry I haven't been in touch more."

"No worries. How are you doing? Is your neck okay?" He squinted at me through his lenses. His face looked drawn, I realized, when I actually got my head out of my ass enough to notice.

"My neck's fine." I should never have lied to him about a pinched nerve. Maybe he knew and that was why he seemed distant. "Are you okay?"

"Yeah, I'm just a little under the weather."

"Still?"

"I'm going to the doctor tomorrow."

"Promise?"

"Yeah."

I told him I would go with him if he wanted and that I would bring him some *tom kha gai,* Thai chicken coconut soup, that night.

"What's this with you and soup?" he said.

"When I was a kid and I got sick, I always wished my mom would make me soup. Or at least pick some up for me."

He said, "You're the sweetest girl in the world, but I don't have much appetite and I've got some leftovers I'm going to eat tonight. And I'm okay to go to the doctor by myself. But maybe you can come by another day after work."

I said okay, but to let me know if he changed his mind about the doctor. He helped Skylar with the weights. Only light ones, Scott insisted, even though Sky wanted to go heavier. Then Sky and I held each other's feet while we did crunches, but he was too ticklish and kept breaking into giggle fits. So we jumped on the trampolines side by side, trying to see who could go higher; he could of course. By the time we were done, I felt much better. While Skylar used the restroom, I hugged Scott and promised I'd see him soon.

He said, "Isn't your birthday coming up?" It was. "You should have a party."

I frowned. "I think that will make it worse. I'd rather just ignore it and hope it goes away."

"Well, I want to celebrate you." Our eyes met. He had long lashes. I used to tease him that it looked like he wore mascara. "You know I just want you to be happy, right?"

"Of course," I said. "Same here."

"And also? Catt?"

I turned back around and he came closer and spoke in a softer voice as if he didn't want anyone else to hear. "I love having you train here because I get to see you. But maybe you want to check out a different gym?"

I knew what he was going to say.

"I know you're not a big fan of Bob's. I've been thinking about what you said. I was kind of preoccupied at the time. But I've been thinking and I think you were right; he doesn't have the best energy for you to be around. Or Skylar. Especially if I'm not here for some reason."

"I told you that a while ago. What changed?"

Scott frowned and I saw the creases deepen in his face. He jammed his hands in his pockets and shifted his weight side to side. "His plastic surgery has gotten way, way out of hand?" Scott's laugh was weak. "I don't know, I just worry more lately."

"I thought that was my job." But I didn't worry enough, then. Not about the right things anyway. Still, I shivered as the cold air blasted my workout-soaked clothes. "What about you? Are you going to try to work somewhere else? Because I'll only bring Skylar on Sundays, but I'm not leaving you."

Scott reached out and squeezed my shoulder. "You won't be," he said.

On the way home Skylar was pensive, staring out the window of the backseat, and I asked him what was on his mind.

"Can we build a Greek temple for my figures tonight?" I'd bought him some Mount Olympus action figures a few weeks earlier. Whatever Sky got into, he did it full on—trains, LEGOs, *Adventure Time*, baseball, now Greek myths.

"Sure, I can get out your old blocks. Do you know the difference between Corinthian and Ionic and Doric columns?"

Of course he did. And the names of all the gods, demigods, and heroes. What a kid. If I ever doubted that the brutal world was also full of magic, he could single-handedly prove me wrong.

"Catt?"

"Yes, Sky?"

"I miss you.

"I miss you, too. I'm sorry I haven't been around as much. I was sad about Dash leaving and I've been dating some guys, but I haven't been choosing them very well, I guess."

I could feel him thinking about it. "But you have people who love you."

"Thank you, sweetie. You're right. I have great people in my life."

"So the next person you go out with has to be like that and treat you really, really well."

Was he thinking about Scott? As I smiled at Skylar in the rearview mirror and blew him a kiss over my shoulder, I realized that no one had said those words to me before. Not even my mom and dad. If anything, they had conveyed the opposite.

One summer my parents and I went to Greece to visit my father's relatives, the Georgiou family. Everyone stayed together in a big house on the island of Crete. During the day my cousins (whom I had never met before) and I hung out on the white-sand-and-clear-blue-water beaches, and at night we all ate dinner together and the parents drank ouzo until they passed out.

It should have been idyllic.

"Go, have fun," my mother had said, practically pushing me out the door one night.

The air smelled like fruit and salt and I could hear the sea, not far away in the dark. I was wearing a white gauze shirt with crocheted butterflies around the neckline and cutoff shorts. My skin was peeling off in pieces from my shoulders and chest from the bad sunburn I'd gotten the first day there.

Where my mother wanted me to *go, have fun* was back to the beach for a bonfire party the cousins were having with some friends. I didn't want to go but I only stood watching as my mother continued to fuss with her blond Swedish hair, pinning it up on her head, pulling out some tendrils, letting it all down again. I wondered about the low-cut, coral-colored dress she was wearing, the toxic sweetness of her perfume. My dad had gone on an overnight trip to Athens with one of his brothers.

"What if someone tries to kiss me?" I finally managed to ask.

"It's the most natural thing in the world," she answered. "Just let it happen."

That wasn't what I meant.

The Greek boys were all dark and curly haired and they paid attention to me, unlike boys at home. It was flattering but also disturbing, and their black-liquid gazes made my stomach quease and my heart pound with fight-or-flight syndrome. Neither of which I did.

One boy—man? he must have been at least eighteen—I don't remember his name, but he resembled the statues of Greek gods I'd seen; his hair spiraled in tight curls and his nose looked as if it had been carved from marble. When I got to the beach, he was sitting by the bonfire, and he stood up and danced, danced, danced with me to the music that was playing, and then he took a gulp of ouzo and kissed me, pouring the licorice fire into my mouth.

I pushed him away and asked if he knew my cousins and he said sure and I was such a beauty and he kissed me again. Then he took my hand and we ran down to the water. It was warm and soft and gleaming, the combination of the waves and the alcohol and *his* beauty and my own low self-esteem made me fall apart in his arms. Next we were back on the sand, away from the party, and he was naked.

I wouldn't let him fuck me so instead he forced me to suck his cock, which I had no idea how to do. He pushed my head down and down again, making me gag, and when he came, I moved away just in time not to get a mouthful. When I stumbled back to my bedroom, I heard laughter from the room next door. I listened through the wall to my mom and my dad's brother-in-law fucking.

"Did you have fun last night?" my mom asked me in the morning.

Fun? My head and jaw ached. A beautiful man had called me beauty and held me in his arms.

Later, I would think, anything could have happened. He could have killed me and chopped me into pieces, eaten me, and no one would have known.

I turned away from her.

I was thirteen.

When I dropped Skylar off, I told Bree what Scott had said about a new gym.

"Why would he say that now?" she asked.

"I have no idea."

Bree shivered. "I can't stand Bob. Maybe we should

stop going there." Then she added, "I thought someone was following me home from the gym the other night. But it's probably my imagination. I'm just on edge lately with everything that's been happening."

I asked her if she wanted me to come inside, even sleep over (it wasn't entirely for her; I could have used more time with Sky and I was anxious not to be alone anyway), but she said no thanks. Something about the way she said it—a little too quickly maybe—made me wonder if she was having a guy over later, but I didn't stop to guess who it might be.

Also, I was more concerned about the idea that someone had possibly been following her. When I got home, I was shaken enough to look behind me a few times as I went up the stairs to my door. I checked all the closets, turned on the alarm, and left the lights on when I went to sleep, with Sasha lying on the bed facing the door like a pretty, petite watchdog.

Scott texted me the next morning: *Seeing you with Skylar at the gym reminded me of how I used to be with my mom. Like you have each other's heart in your hands. I love you. PS There's a special at SilverTone Gym.*

"Each other's heart in your hands." I knew that saying Sky and I reminded Scott of his mother and him was a big compliment. I sent him a heart emoji, *Don't worry,* and an *xoxo.* That's all.

Why hadn't I been able to fall in love with sweet,

sweet Scott? Was it because no one had told me that I deserved someone who treated me "really, really well"? Was it because he wasn't a tall, tatted "artist"? I was an idiot, basically. And still, even at that late—just before too late—date, enough of one not to do anything about it.

#10

I did take Scott's advice about having a party, though. Without telling Bree, I got Botox from her ex-Vampire, who assured me I wasn't starting too early, that many of his patients were already getting injections in their twenties.

As he prepared to stick the needle in with his long, pale hands, I said, "I have a high tolerance for physical pain but not for emotional." Too much information.

He looked down at me blankly with his blue-ice eyes that contrasted with his black hair. "Good," he said. "Because this is going to hurt."

But he didn't warn me that it was going to bruise. Bree never bruised. Mine were bad—dark smudges. I covered them with thick makeup, but my clients at work kept saying I had something on my face and one lady even tried to rub the bruises off. I wondered if they'd be gone by my party. I had this idea that I had to look good that night, in case Dean showed up.

Because I had stooped low enough to invite him. Yes, I realized he was an asshole who had fucked me and then disappeared. Yes, I was aware that I was moving my pain about being alone around from man to man. No, I couldn't stop.

He had e-mailed me back saying he was sorry he'd been out of touch, he'd been on a book tour and just going through a lot and he would try to make it. I wished I didn't give a shit whether he came or not.

On the night of my party, my bruises still showed under the makeup. I'd prepared lasagna, salad and non-alcoholic tiramisu, hoping to distract everyone from my appearance with my culinary talents. There was also the distraction of organic red wine and rum punch for the folks who drank. I lit candles, hoping to hide in the dim. I played music loud, hoping to hide in the din. It didn't work.

Scott came by early, gave me a quick kiss, said he wasn't feeling great but he loved me and was so glad I'd taken his advice and thrown myself a party—I deserved one. I wanted to tell him what was going on with me but it felt selfish since he wasn't in such great shape himself. So when he left I went to find Shana for some moral support, but Bree said she had a headache and went home early, too.

"She wished you a happy birthday," Bree told me.

I told Bree that I was freaked out. Ashamed that I'd invited Dean. Ashamed of the bruises on my face. She dragged me into the bathroom and plastered more makeup on me. The foundation was cakey and thick and I stared at the mask in the mirror.

We went back out and I refilled some people's drinks. The alcohol fumes made me a little dizzy. I remembered I hadn't eaten, but then I got busy talking to Todd and Rick and forgot.

I checked my cell phone. Dean hadn't texted—no surprise.

Stu showed. Surprise. He had come back to the salon after our encounter, and Bree forced him to pay and apologize to me. I apologized for nicking him. That was that, except for the surge of nausea I felt whenever I thought of him—much like smelling sausage pizza from which I had once contracted food poisoning as a child.

What the fuck? He told me that he'd overheard us talking about the party and he wanted to come and make a peace offering. Kendra had given him my address. Why would she do that?

"You have something on your face," Stu said, handing me a plate covered in aluminum foil.

"Yeah," I said. "I know."

I turned around and bumped into the chest of a tall man in a pressed white dress shirt; he was holding a large bouquet of roses with gradient petals shaded from white to pink to red. I looked up at his strong jawline. It was Cyan. My chest was full of flowers.

"Happy birthday," he said.

"Why are you here?"

He smiled with the dark blueness of his eyes. "I came by to surprise you and saw all the activity. I hope you don't mind."

"No," I said. "I'm glad you're here."

"I can't stay long. I'm just passing through. But I wanted to bring you these." He handed me the flowers and I thanked him.

Bree came up. "Do you want me to put those in water?" She was staring at Cyan. He nodded at her. "They're beautiful," she said.

He turned back to me. "Have you eaten anything yet?"

"I was too excited."

"You should eat." He took me over to the table and I took a chocolate chip cookie from a plate someone had set there. It tasted sweet and dense. I thought of Cyan's mouth on mine, his cock touching my cervix. I didn't want him to leave.

"Want to dance?" I asked him.

He shook his head. "I don't dance. You go dance."

Ladytron was blasting something electronic and spacey. I took Bree's hand—she was still watching Cyan intently—and pulled her into the middle of the living room to dance the way we used to in the clubs, close and sexy so the men would notice us. Or, I guess, me, because they would have noticed her anyway. Maybe Cyan would watch me dance. I thought of taking off my heels but decided I'd look better with them on even if my feet hurt. My silk dress—the one I'd worn the night Dash left and not since—was wet with sweat.

We danced a long time. Then Bree wasn't there. I was dancing with Deirdre, the anorexic model. I couldn't remember Deirdre being there before? She looked so thin I wondered how she could stand up, let alone dance. There were bruises all over her bare legs. I thought, *There is a skeleton of pain beneath your flesh and I can see it.*

Everyone is in pain.

Where was Cyan? Where was Bree? I stopped dancing and went to find her. Todd and Rick were standing in the hall. They looked hollow eyed like they were discussing the end of the world. I thought, *They're going to break up tonight. And there's nothing I can do about it.* I tried to explain to them that something was terribly wrong but I couldn't articulate. . . . In fact, I was having trouble speaking.

Where was Bree? Why had Shana left? I wondered if she was mad at me. Maybe she thought I shouldn't have served alcohol. My blood hurt.

I checked my cell phone. Dean had left a message. The pain in my body lessened as if someone had sucked it away with a big straw, or pulled it out with their teeth. Until I read the text: *Got caught up with something. Hope you had a happy birthday.*

Pain crashed through me again. I'd more than half expected this from Dean, but I had also really wanted the escape. I texted him back: *U r a manticore.* I thought, *Where's Cyan? Maybe he left. That would be a bad idea anyway. I am falling in love with him; never sleep with a man you are falling in love with. Wait, that doesn't sound right . . . I should text Jarell.* But I suddenly couldn't figure out how to send a text.

My mouth was so dry it felt like cake mix.

I had to find Bree.

There she was. Looking at me with too-big eyes. I could see every pore, every tiny line in her face. (She was due for her Botox and I had fewer lines than she did for once.) I could feel the pain in her blood, too. It was threatening to take her over. She was angry at me.

"Are you fucked-up?" she shouted.

I backed away. *I'm fucked-up. How did I get fucked-up?* I needed to sit down, but where was the couch? I recognized that I was in my house, but why was that wall there? Where was the front door?

I found a couch and sat. Was it my couch? I was sinking into it as if I weighed three hundred pounds. Where were my shoes? Why was everyone in so much pain? Pain was everywhere in the world. It never stopped.

Toddrick was sitting next to me, asking if I was okay. I wanted to tell them to take me to the hospital but I couldn't make my mouth form words.

"Did you take something?" they said.

I shook my head no. It took all the strength I had. I wanted water but I didn't know how to ask for it.

"Did someone give you something? What did you eat?"

I thought for a long, long time. I'd cooked all day. Cooked, cooked, cooked. I hadn't eaten. Anything. Except. The cookie. I tried to tell Toddrick. Or Ricktodd?

But I couldn't speak. There was dry cake-mix powder in the pockets of my cheeks. Or something.

Someone was sitting next to me but I couldn't turn my head to look. Then the person leaned forward. It was Deirdre. Her face was too big. Her lips were like fruit hanging off a tree. She said, "You're high. Just go with it. It can be awesome. Really. You'll look back at this and be like, 'I want to do that again.'"

I tried to tell her that I was an addict and I couldn't get high. How many years had I been sober? I tried to count them but I kept getting confused and starting over again. Where was Bree? I wanted someone to get her for me.

Then she was yelling, "I can't believe she would do that. She just went and blew eleven fucking years? What the fuck." Her face loomed out of the darkness at me, raging.

She was talking about me. I was "she." But it wasn't my fault. I had to explain.

"You need to lie down," someone said. It was Kendra.

I tried to ask her about Stu. Had she really given him my address? It didn't make any sense. I couldn't speak. She smelled like raw honey and her hands were soft. There wasn't pain hiding in her bones or hanging off her shoulders like a coat. Tenderness. Happiness. She helped me up and walked me to my bedroom. I wondered if she would stay and lie with me. Once she had put her hands between my legs. But that had hurt, too. And it wasn't sex. I wanted my mommy.

I wanted Shana.

I wanted Scott.

I wanted Cyan—*no, I mean Dash*. No, Cyan.

No. The person I really, really wanted was Bree.

But Bree, too, was more gone than I knew.

In the morning she came into the room like the sun, hurting my eyes. Her hair was back in a high, tight ponytail and she had fresh makeup on her face. "You look like shit," she shouted.

"I'm sorry," I said, cowering.

"I've been up all night cleaning the mess." Her eyes flared like gas flames.

"I didn't know," I said. "There were cookies with something in them."

"What cookies? You ate cookies?" If her eyes could make a sound, they would have shrieked like sirens. She pulled her hair out of the ponytail, smoothed it, put the ponytail holder back in again. There was a red mark on her wrist where the ponytail band had recently been.

"I think Stu brought them," I said. Each word was like spitting a cotton ball out of my overstuffed mouth. "There was a plate with foil."

"If Stu did that, don't you think someone else would have gotten high? And I didn't see any cookies anyway."

"They were there!"

Bree ignored me and surveyed the room. "The house

looks great," she said. "I was up all night." Her voice was shrill.

I got out of bed and followed her into the kitchen, shuffling my heavy animal feet. There were trash bags lined up neatly by the door, and the floor had been mopped clean. The only thing she hadn't done was touch the bottles of rum and wine. They stood on the table fermenting. I picked one up to pour it into the sink.

"Don't touch anything," Bree snapped. "You're still high. You'll make a mess."

"I'm sure this was kind of triggering," I said. "I'm really sorry."

Bree's mom was a complete mess, addicted to the pain pills she took after her many plastic surgeries. So, growing up, Bree kept the house clean and herself looking perfect. She learned how to do hair and makeup, take photos and arrange flowers; she designed and made her clothes. That had been the way she dealt with things. And then she started to drink and use as a way to deal with things, but she still always managed to have a clean house and great hair, makeup, and clothes.

"You must be angry. But I didn't know . . ."

"I'm not angry," Bree said. "Don't tell me what I feel, Catt."

"I'm sorry," I said.

"Just get back to bed. You'll break something."

"I'm going to take a shower." But I just stood there. I felt like I should eat, but the thought of the leftover lasagna and soggy salad Bree had wrapped in plastic and put in the fridge made me sick, and there wasn't much else. I got some water, but Bree seemed to want me out of the kitchen as soon as possible. The hell out. Of my kitchen.

"You'll probably have some flashbacks for a few days," she said as I slippered my way to my room, head hanging. "You'll lose things, forget things and shit. Good luck at work Tuesday."

Bree left a few hours later, after she had done the laundry and scrubbed the bathroom with bleach. I kept telling her I was okay and she should go rest but she ignored me. "Go lie down," Bree kept saying. "You are so still high."

I hated Sunday nights. Even though I didn't work Mondays, Sunday nights were this blackness encroaching, spreading inside of me. Maybe it was left over from being in school. That night was worse. I was thirty-seven, alone, still fucked-up. I had lost my sobriety. My eleven years. Lost, like a child who had been abducted, taken from me. I would have to start all over again. But how could I start over?

Bree wouldn't listen to my explanation if I had even been able to articulate what had happened—what I *thought* had happened. She didn't pick up anyway so I texted her, *I'm sorry. I didn't know. I don't know what else to say.* I called Shana but she didn't answer. Wondered (paranoid-ly?) if Bree and her had decided to avoid me together. I thought of calling Dash and decided not to. I could not call Cyan. I knew I'd never call Dean again. Dean, saying all that shit about me *being his*. *If he had come you wouldn't have eaten that cookie.* No, that wasn't true. The getting high was my fault. And maybe Stu's if he'd brought those cookies. Who else would have brought them? There wasnt anyone I could talk to about it. I didn't want to bother Scott. Finally I settled on Jarell. I don't know why. Maybe because he wasn't my best friend, my sponsor, my ex, my ex's brother. (*I'm just passing through.* Cyan, Cyan. Who once told me, "Your face is so full of love.") But Jarell had never pretended to care. Yet, maybe he did in some way. Just about me as a person, a friend? Could that be? I convinced myself, yes, a little, and hit the contact.

He didn't answer.

I texted him.

He texted back, *I'm at a family function. Can't speak now. Everything okay?*

I couldn't help it; I called again. What an asshole I was being. Jarell answered.

When I heard his voice, I started to cry. Yes, for real. He asked what was wrong. I heard people in the background. I apologized. I told him that I'd had a party and something happened.

He said, "What happened?" His voice was deep and muscular and soft.

I told him that someone gave me cookies and I ate one and got wasted.

Jarell said, "You scared me there. That's all it was? I thought you were going to say someone took advantage of you. And I'd have to beat the shit out of them."

This made me cry more.

Jarell said, "See, this is what I'm talking about. With your godson. How are you going to teach him to live in this world if you cry like this at everything."

"I'm sorry," I said. "But my best friend, she's so angry."

"Listen, I gotta go. Someday you'll look back at this and it won't seem so bad," he said. Before he hung up.

I had made a mistake about Jarell. Booty call or not, at least he had cared about Skylar. At least Jarell had wanted to see me again. I was the one who had said no. And now there was nothing between us except this humiliating phone call.

There was a text from Bree: *Stop saying you are sorry. You don't have to tell me you are sorry anymore. How about saying thank you for helping me? For staying up all night cleaning my house and making sure I was okay? I can't be there for you anymore. I can't trust you with my son. I won't see you at work on Tuesday. Shana got me a job at this salon her friend just opened.*

Sunday night wasn't all that bad. Compared to this, I'd have welcomed an eternity of Sunday nights. Now I know better, I guess.

Shana went with me to a meeting Monday morning. She told me to share, but I could not bring myself to say the words out loud: "I went out. I lost eleven years." Even if it had been unintentional, I didn't know if anyone would believe me.

After, at Planet Pie, Shana said that Bree had come over on Sunday "completely freaked-out," and that Shana thought it best for Bree and me not to be in touch for awhile.

I stared into my coffee cup. "But I didn't know." I looked up at Shana, sitting across the linoleum-topped table. She was tan from a weekend in Palm Springs, and Bree had given her a Brazilian blowout so her hair, straightened, reached her waist. My voice was rising up like bile in my throat. "I didn't know!"

"It's not just what happened at the party, Catt. Your behavior's been erratic and she's not strong enough to handle it. She loves you too much to have to watch you going through this."

Loves me too much? I wanted to scream at Shana, scream at Bree. Instead I swallowed it like a pill. But the pill stuck in my throat. And I needed Jack to wash it down.

When I went into the salon Tuesday, Bree really wasn't there. Kendra hugged me and asked if I was okay.

I said, "Why'd you give Stu my address?"

"Shit. I'm sorry. He told me you invited him and he misplaced the e-mail. I wondered why you would have invited him. He said he wanted to apologize for being an asshole."

I looked up Stu's number and called him. Surprisingly he answered.

"This is Catt," I said.

"Hey, Catt."

"Did you bring cookies to my party?" I asked.

"Uh, no. Why?"

"Someone brought weed Monster cookies. THC. Whatever. I'm sober," I said. "I was."

"Oh, man, that sucks."

"It doesn't suck. It's fucking serious. Why did you lie to Kendra about me inviting you? What the fuck is wrong with you?"

"Man," he said. "Get some help, will you?" And hung up.

#11

There was a pall. It was the first time I understood the word. A pall over everything. They were all standing around—Rick and Todd and even Big Bob, who never stops moving, who never just stands there. They were speaking quietly and the music was playing as usual, but very, very softly so you could hardly hear. Some stupid pop ditty, the kind you can't get out of your head; you might even wake in the middle of the night singing it in your sleep. Something about how someone doesn't understand how shining and special you are, and that you are going to go dance in a club and wave your hands in the air and have a "drank" and show everyone the truth! I was thinking that I liked nineties music so much more. And then I saw Scott's photo on the counter.

It didn't make sense. I like Scott's face. I just looked at it, in the photo, smiling.

The quiet seemed to get quieter. A vein twitched in

Bob's neck. Rick stepped closer. I didn't want to hear what he was going to tell me.

"What?" I said anyway.

"Catt, Scott died," Rick said. His voice had slowed way down and it sounded too deep.

I stepped back. I moved away from them. I had to be away from them. I tried to walk to the door to leave, and then I circled back and kept walking around and around.

"What are you talking about?" I said. "I just saw him. He had the flu."

"Early this morning. He called an ambulance and he died at the hospital," someone said.

I think it was Rick but I couldn't tell. They were all mumbling. Todd had his hands folded in front of him as if he were trying to keep them from running away.

"He called an ambulance? What was wrong? He didn't call me. I was going to bring him dinner tonight."

I couldn't breathe. I walked back to the door so that the bell chimed a warning, and then back to them. "What happened? He had the flu," I said. I might have been screaming.

Todd took my hand and walked me outside, past Scott, smiling in the picture. In the cruel sunlight Todd was pale under his spray tan. There were some palm trees. They were too tall and ragged. I wanted to climb up and trim them properly.

"He had leukemia," Todd said.

"What?" I said. "He wasn't feeling well. He had a flu."

Todd tried to touch me and I had to keep myself from hitting him. I backed away. He said my name. He had bags under his eyes like he hadn't slept.

"When did you find out?"

"They called us at two in the morning. It was too late."

"They called you. They didn't call me." I said it as if it were just a bunch of words that didn't mean anything. That didn't mean *Scott is dead, he had leukemia, he didn't let me know, he didn't call me to take him to the hospital, he didn't have them call me, they called Todd and Rick, he died alone.*

"It was too late. He could hardly get to the hospital. Everything had shut down."

I walked back inside the gym as if I would find him there with his hands in his pockets, laughing at himself. Rick said, "Catt?"

"Scott had leukemia," I said.

Rick said, "Nobody knew except his mom. He found out a year ago but he didn't want to tell anyone. He didn't want to upset us and he refused treatment."

I looked at Scott's smiling picture. Someone had downloaded it from his Facebook profile. It was an old picture because more recently he had been looking a little thinner—peaked—and he didn't like having his picture taken. He said his immune system was down a bit. He had had the flu. I was going to bring him food. I was going to make it and bring it over to his house. I had taken the picture at a Dodger game we'd gone to with Skylar, Bree, some guy she was dating, and Rick and Todd. Scott looked tan, muscular, wearing a Dodger cap, the field bathed in purple summer-evening light behind him. His jawline was defined. He had a nice jaw. He wasn't smiling too widely, hiding his teeth, though he had good teeth. But at that moment I couldn't remember his teeth.

That day Scott and I hung out at his place after everyone else had left. Dash had a band rehearsal and I didn't feel like being alone. We were sitting on the couch, wearing socks, watching TV, and eating Chinese food out of cartons that we handed back and forth.

"See?" he'd said, gesturing around the tiny apartment, which was bigger than the studio he'd moved into. (*To die*, I realized.) "If you'd married me, you could have had all this." He was smiling but only with the edges of his mouth.

I put my hand on his chest without thinking about it. "I could have had this," I said.

"You have that anyway. You always will."

Not anymore.

What Scott had was leukemia and he hadn't told me. It made me feel that I didn't know anything about him; he was someone gone whom I had never known. Underneath the photo it said, *Our Friend Scott Steadman: In Loving Memory.*

I went back outside again. I couldn't stop moving

around, up and down the street in front of Body Farm. No one followed me this time. I took out my cell phone and called Bree. She didn't answer. She never did. Even then.

My mom died of cancer, too, but at that point we were estranged. I heard from a family friend that she died alone in a hospice.

Sometimes I remembered how, when we lived in the apartment in North Hollywood, after my dad left, my mom would call me into her bed, saying she was afraid to sleep alone. There might be murderers out there, she had said. Serial killers like Richard Ramirez, the Night Stalker, who broke through windows and raped and murdered women when I was a little girl. Her pale skin was clammy and her breath stank of alcohol.

Sometimes I would imagine her dying, then. How I would have to hold her hand until her heart stopped beating, how I would have to change her clothes when it did, what her corpse would feel like in my arms. I had never held a corpse in my arms, but I would have held Scott. I would have undressed him and put him in fresh clothes. I would have combed his hair. I would have kissed his mouth. I would have slept next to him all night until they made me let them take him away.

That night I got his mother's number from Rick, who had Scott's cell phone. I was surprised when she answered.

"This is Scott's friend, Catt," I said. "We spoke on the phone before."

"Hello, Catt." Her voice was strained and hoarse but she wasn't sobbing. That Midwestern stoicism always amazed me.

"I loved him so much," I said. "Once he told me that the way I was with my friend's son reminded him of how you were with him as a kid. It was such a high compliment."

She thanked me.

I wanted to ask more about the illness and why he kept it a secret, why he refused to treat it, but I couldn't bring myself to ask. If she cried, I was afraid I'd start sobbing.

"I'm so, so sorry." I stopped to swallow back the lump congealing in my throat. "Please let me know if there's anything I can do."

Of course, there is never anything anyone can do.

She thanked me again, told me to take care, and hung up.

Take care of yourself. What I couldn't seem to learn to do. The lump in my throat exploded into a shuddering gasp. Where was Scott? It was as if he had been cut out of me with a dull kitchen knife.

I tried to put together the pieces of the puzzle of his illness. The mysterious surgery he'd had on his leg in his early twenties, the fevers, the fatigue, the breakup with

Emi, the way he had distanced himself from me and Bree and even Skylar. Why hadn't I pushed him to tell me more about himself and what he was going through?

Scott's funeral was going to be in Ohio and only the immediate family was invited, so Rick and Todd had a reception to honor him. They lived in a large Spanish house in the hills. We walked up the steep stairs to the terra-cotta-tiled patio decorated with potted palms. The hot desert winds had kicked up, running fingers through the fronds. Past French doors a lavish brunch buffet was spread on a heavy oak table. No one seemed to have much of an appetite. I stared into the flames of the gardenia candles burning everywhere and wondered where Scott had gone.

Bree and Skylar hadn't come yet. Emi was there, looking whitewashed, like someone in chronic physical pain. She was wearing Scott's death like a black coat that was too heavy for her.

As I hugged her gymnast's body, I felt a slam of guilt that I'd been jealous when Scott and she first hooked up. I'd secretly disparaged him for picking such a young woman. But I hadn't wanted him for myself (stupid me), even if I was single at the time and he had pursued me, so what right did I have to judge his choices? She was lovely; I could see why he'd picked her. And I knew that he had broken up with her because he hadn't wanted her to deal with her boyfriend dying. That any distance he had created between himself and me was probably nothing to do with her and all about his own gradual withdrawal from the world.

"He never told me," she said, shaking her shiny black ponytail from side to side. "Did he ever tell you?"

"No. Only his mom. I'm so sorry, Emi."

"Do you know how I found out? No one called me. The day after it happened I went on his Facebook page to see if he was dating someone and I saw all these posts." Tears slid down her high, rounded cheekbones. "Leukemia?" she said. "Who does that? Lets themself die of leukemia? Doesn't get treatment. He was so selfish. So vain. Was it because he didn't want to lose his hair or something?" She started to sob and I held her until she quieted. I'd thought the same thing about Scott, at first, but I knew it wasn't that simple. He hadn't wanted to cause anyone any trouble, and what bigger trouble could he cause than getting cancer, going through the treatments, and then maybe dying right away anyway? I didn't tell all this to Emi, though. It would be easier if she believed Scott was selfish and vain, at least for that day.

Emi left soon after, and Todd called for us all to gather in the living room and told a story about how when he first met Scott, everyone assumed he was gay. "Because he was so well groomed, sensitive, and thoughtful." Everyone chuckled. "Then I realized he was just an amazing person and that everyone should be more gay." He read the last text Scott had sent him. *You're doing so great with your workouts. Keep it up, buddy. Love you, man.*

Todd shook his head and bit his lip. "Sorry. I just wish I'd seen that as a good-bye."

It turned out everyone had a good-bye text from Scott that they hadn't realized was one. We began an impromptu read of them. All of the messages had a special, personal reference and the words *I love you.* I read mine but stopped at the PS about him not wanting me to go to Body Farm anymore.

It hadn't occurred to me until that moment that Bob wasn't at the gathering. *Come to think of it, neither is Leila. And Bree's still not here.*

I needed her then, and Skylar, but she didn't respond to my text. I almost e-mailed Sky but decided it wouldn't be cool to do that until I heard from her. So I left.

At about three in the morning I woke to a knocking sound and a man's voice whispering, "I am here."

I bolted up; my dreams never had soundtracks like that. Outside, the Santa Anas tossed branches against the glass. So it had been the wind? Sasha had moved to the windowsill and was staring out into darkness. She looked, and felt—when I touched her—electric. *I thought someone was following me home the other night,* Bree had said. Was that someone out there? Following her, following us?

I reached for the phone.

The cops came forty minutes later. Two tall men with rock-hard chests. The older one was especially hugely muscled with acne scars scattered over his angular bone structure. The younger, baby-faced one had darker skin and bright green eyes. I wished they would both just move in with me. *Or at least stay the night.*

"What seems to be the trouble, ma'am?" the older one said. His name tag read RODRIGUEZ. I was holding Sasha over my chest as if I hadn't changed out of my nightgown and put on a bra.

I told him about the knock on my door but not about the whisper I'd heard. They checked the perimeter of the house, said to make sure to keep everything locked up tight. I admitted I was more on edge than usual with the Hollywood Serial Killer out there, especially since my neighbor had been killed. I didn't mention the dissolution of my marriage, the death of my best friend. Scott had told me once that he wanted to be a cop but his leg surgery had prevented it. I could imagine him standing there in a crew cut and uniform, taking care of me, taking care of people.

"Yeah, we'll all sleep better when we catch him," the younger cop said. CORONADO. "Meanwhile you just need to keep your eyes open and your windows shut."

Sasha jumped out of my arms and began circling their feet, her tail wrapping their legs as if she, too, wanted them to stay. "My watch cat," I said. "She likes you." I was pathetic.

They nodded, kept their arms crossed, patted their

biceps, and left. But the younger officer turned back, handed me his card, leaning in so I could smell his cologne. "Take it easy and call if you need anything," he said.

I picked Sasha up again and got in bed, where I counted my lives in order to fall asleep. Or rather, deaths. Dash and Darcy London. Jarell. Carlton. Dean. Cyan. Scott was number six. I only had three more to go.

#12

My seventh death was in the shape of a key. My house key, in a Bubble Wrap envelope with Bree's handwriting scrawled across the front in hot-pink Sharpie. There was no note.

I called her, I texted, I e-mailed, but there was no response. I said, and typed, again and again, that someone had laced the cookies with THC, that I had no idea, that I would never have eaten one.

Now I was supposed to go to meetings and call Shana every day, but I was blistering with resentment and I didn't want to talk to her at all. I went to work and tried to pretend I was okay. The owners had hired my client Karli to replace Bree. She spent the entire day talking about her husband. He still didn't know she had hair extensions.

"How's Bree?" Karli asked on a break from hubby talk. "Why'd she quit? Aren't you besties?"

"She got a job somewhere else," I said, hoping to shut her down with my grim expression.

I don't think it was necessarily my face but rather Karli's desire to return to the subject of her man that got me off the hook about Bree.

At night I drove past the corner liquor store and stared at the poster of the woman with the bottle between her breasts.

Hungry. Angry. Lonely. Tired. I was all four. It seemed I always was. I ate a salad and took a cool shower and tried to sleep, but the nights were so hot and I couldn't open the windows. All I wanted was to see Skylar's face. If I closed my eyes, I could imagine it so clearly—the soiled baseball cap, the cheeks flushed, the eyes lit green. Sometimes I couldn't look at baby photos of him; it was just too much—those fat cheeks and dimples and the gold curls tumbling down. When had he slimmed out and grown such straight, thick brown hair? Now his school photo at the salon made me feel the same cringe of pain. He didn't have a phone I could call so Bree wouldn't know. And I couldn't do that anyway. It was one thing to lose Dash and Bree, but Skylar? I hadn't realized how he'd single-handedly held the space between me and my desire to die.

That night I crawled in bed and watched the worst reality TV I could find. Sasha hid as if it offended her. On these shows there were all kinds of men behaving badly, but I realized that I might not have recognized it until the shows pointed it out. Had I learned more from reality TV than from my own mom and dad? Men were supposed to pay for the first dates, wait to try to sleep with you, express interest in you, not just what you looked like. Parents weren't supposed to encourage hookups between their teenage daughters and twenty-one-year-old men. Fathers were supposed to tell their daughters to put on more clothes and to quiz their prospective boyfriends at the door. To protect their daughters from danger.

"Too late," I said to the screen. The numbness had just started to set in.

But not enough.

The phone rang. It was Todd. I hadn't seen him in a while, since I'd been avoiding the gym. He said, "Put on the local news." I turned the channel. Leila's face was there. A head shot. And some candid shots of her laughing and without much makeup so her freckles showed. It hit me with a dull, blunt-object thud in my chest.

Todd was still talking. She had been gone since we had the gathering for Scott. Actually, before that. Since before Scott's death. Everyone figured she had just been out of town. But she still wasn't back and she hadn't returned anyone's calls.

"They found her body in the desert," Todd said. "She was . . ." He stopped. He was crying.

"No." I wanted to hang up.

"Her breasts were—"

"No," I repeated.

"—cut off. Do you want us to come over?"

"No."

"Catt?"

"I have to hang up," I said.

I drove to the liquor store that night and purchased a bottle of Jack Daniel's. Then I went home and got in the bathtub and drank the whole thing. It was not dramatic in any way. I just drank it down. I did not call Shana or Bree or Dash or Cyan or Jarell. Instead, I stayed up all night and googled Leila Reynolds. So many pretty pictures of her. Clicking through them, it was as if I was looking for some clue, but I had no idea what I was really looking for. Until I found it.

There was a picture of Leila in shorts and a crop top, her hair straightened so that it looked even longer and shinier, working out at Body Farm. Around her neck she was wearing a gold necklace that spelled out one word: *California*.

When I tried to stand up, I watched the room circle me like a carousel. Or a zoopraxiscope. Was that what it was called? Those early viewing machines that predated movies? Determined, I got up anyway—though a muscle spasm in my hip clawed me back—and tried to walk to the bathroom but almost fell. A metallic taste swam up my gullet. I vomited on the floor and for a moment felt a bitter relief.

Who had been in my house who knew Leila? Who

had been on my couch? From whose pocket could the necklace have slipped? Bree was always here, but Bree was gone now. Scott and I had eaten Chinese food recently on my couch. Scott had been Leila's trainer before Big Bob took over. I could see a man standing over Leila with blood splattering his glasses, glazing his hands. Killing all those women as if somehow by taking their lives he could lengthen his own. Because he had nothing to lose? What was I thinking? I was thinking that Scott was a killer?

I went to look for the California necklace in my jewelry box but it wasn't there. The last time I'd seen it was when I'd photographed it for my *Love Monster* blog, draped over blue satin with a vintage 1950s *Visit California* postcard in the background.

I picked up the phone and called the North East police station, asking for Officer Coronado, the cop who had given me his card. A female officer answered and told me he wasn't available. "May I help you?"

"I think I may have some information about a case," I said. "The woman who was killed? Leila Reynolds. I had her necklace. But I didn't know that it was hers. Someone left it in my couch. Then they took it."

I must have sounded drunk and crazy because the officer only took down my name and number and told me someone would contact me in the morning.

#

The next day Officer Coronado called me back. In spite of, or maybe because of, the circumstances, my heart fluttered like a true-love addict's when I heard his voice. As if he might rescue me from all of this.

I told the officer that I'd last seen Leila Reynolds at the gym. That Bob was her trainer. That she was very sweet and everyone seemed to like her. No boyfriend that I knew of. No local, immediate family. That I knew of. I didn't tell him this: that I had assumed things about her because she was nice and beautiful. I had assumed she was loved and happy.

"Do you have any suspects?"

"I'm sorry, we can't divulge that information," the officer said. "You mentioned something about a necklace on the phone?"

I wanted a drink. To put out the wildfire inside of me. "I found it between the cushions in my couch. It looked like the one she was wearing in a picture I saw online. It said *California*. But now it's gone. Do you want to see a photo? On my blog. I could show you."

"So you say you found this item in your couch? Where is it now?"

"I don't know," I said. "I think maybe someone took it. It was in my jewelry box and then it was gone." The idea of Scott, the would-be cop, being involved with Leila's death, taking her necklace and leaving it in my couch, seemed insane in the light, which is why I did not mention him then. But why had the necklace been there? If it had been there at all?

"I'm so sorry, ma'am. I know this is a stressful time. But I'd imagine there are thousands of these type of necklaces, and I can't really do anything without some actual evidence. I'll be honest with you, this isn't going to go anywhere, but if it would make you feel better, I'd be more than happy to take a report."

"Thank you," I said, flooded with a tide of red shame that included suspecting Scott, wasting the officer's time, and wanting to smell his cologne again. "It's okay. I'm sorry."

On the way home from work that night I bought some more Jack and drank it, welcoming the burn in my throat, the way my head spun. Then I went online and typed in *Hollywood Serial Killer*. I stared at the photos of the victims. Mandy Merrill. Adrienne Banks. Michelle Babcock. Leila Reynolds. They all had long hair, long legs, big eyes, big breasts. My brain hurt as I rummaged roughly through it, searching.

They all looked like someone else.

They all looked like Bree.

The pictures on my phone were mostly of Bree and me at work when we got bored. Of our hair. The styles we gave each other. Bree couldn't take a bad photograph, from either side of the camera, actually. Even when she'd been a full-blown addict, she always looked perfect in every shot. I came to a picture of Skylar and me that she'd taken. We were both leaning out the windows of her SUV, wearing aviator sunglasses and backward Dodger caps and scowling unconvincingly, smiles lurking underneath. Then there was a picture of Bree and Skylar leaning on each other, back-to-back, with their arms crossed over their chests. Badass. Bree. Who looked like Leila and the others.

And someone had followed Bree home from the gym one night.

I knew then that Bree was in danger. Worse than the danger I was in from myself.

I drove the few short blocks to Bree's apartment building. When I drank, I thought I was a pretty good driver—more relaxed. Yes, I actually told myself this. I put on NPR to help me relax more. There was a story about a tiny Egyptian statue in a museum in England that moved incrementally in a perfect circle all by itself. No one knew how it did this. I wondered if it was some sign of the end of the world.

Sleeping morning glories and insomniac jasmine clambered up the adobe walls and over the tiled roof of the building. The summer air smelled oversweet, as if it were trying to lure me somewhere unsafe. A large, sinister-looking banana tree blocked the front window. All lights were off inside.

Bree and Skylar lived on the ground floor; I had always hated that. Now more than ever.

I knocked on the wooden door, and then on the glass panel on top, knowing no one would answer. No one did. Maybe Bree was out on a date or at a meeting with

Shana, and Skylar was with Baby Daddy. *Skylar should
be with me.*

Not now, you're fucked-up.

Before Bree and I were sober, we used to have parties at
this apartment building. We served cheap white wine
in plastic glasses and chugged whiskey from our pri-
vate stash. We wore tutus and off-the-shoulder span-
dex shirts or corsets, cropped lace leggings, and combat
boots. Our hair was cut in bangs and styled in braids.

One party had a wedding theme, and for that we
wore bridal dresses we had found at a thrift store,
hemmed into minis and dyed bright pink. We put white
sheets over the picnic table in the yard and decorated it
with candles and roses in jam jars. The food was a buffet
of cheeses, chocolate, and grapes. Blue twinkle lights in
the trees. Some friend of someone's played the harp. Bree
and I stood on her neighbor's balcony and pretended to
get married. Then we threw our bouquets of roses down
into the garden, and Baby Daddy dove and caught them
both. No one knew who he was, but he was tall and tan
with slanted, green eyes, had surfed professionally, and
was in a band, so he was allowed to stay. I sucked his
comely cock while he went down on Bree. He tasted
like citrus and his skin was ridiculously soft. Then she
kicked him out and she and I slept in each other's arms
in her four-poster bed with our dyed-pink wedding
veils hanging from the wrought-iron chandelier.

This happened another time, this threesome, on one of the very last nights Bree and I got wasted. The night Baby Daddy fucked me, and then Bree, and Skylar was conceived. The death of the Barbicide boy and Bree's pregnancy had sobered Bree and me up almost immediately after that, and we never slept in the same bed again.

Now, staring up at that balcony, I realized that Bree had not only been my best friend. The mother of my darling. The lens through which I saw the beauty of the world. She had been my wife.

I had to protect her, not just for her own sake, and for mine. I had to keep her safe for Skylar.

A cool night breeze whispered chillingly into the back of my neck. "I am here." Was he here? The man who had killed and mutilated all those women? Including Leila. The man who had followed Bree home. What if that was the same man? What if he was going to kill Bree and chop off parts of her?

I turned and vomited into the bushes.

The next day I had a hangover and the shakes and no clients anyway so I decided to call in sick. Besides, I had to see Skylar. I had to. Maybe I'd go see Bree when she got home from work, I told myself. Make sure she was okay. Warn her.

I drove to the baseball field wearing sunglasses and a cap. The empty baseball diamond radiated heat so the little boys had moved under the shade of some trees. Sweat trickled down my sides as I watched the kids stretching with Jarell, facing someone I couldn't see. Jarell looked taller and bigger than before, so gorgeous, but I didn't care. Where was Sky?

When I spotted him, he became all I saw. Walking back from the restrooms wearing his Dodgers cap. I wanted to run to him so much it made my heart feel like it was a pile of sand, collapsing in on itself.

Then I realized that I *could* go to him here. I could just tell Jarell that I'd come by to say hi. He wouldn't know about the fallout between Bree and me.

I got out of the car and started to walk toward them. My heart had reassembled itself and was beating solidly against the emptiness of my body. Jarell looked up and frowned at me. I thought, *Shit, he thinks I'm hitting on him or something.*

Maybe this was a mistake. But I couldn't turn back.

Skylar was running toward me. I almost fell to my knees. He hugged me but not the way he used to. More reserved. Maybe because the other kids were watching. And he was bigger now—taller. He'd grown since I'd last seen him. His eyes shifted away from mine. But all that mattered was that I was hugging him. Still . . . I wondered if I smelled like drink. Was that why he wasn't holding me as tightly? Fuck, I couldn't let him see me cry.

And then it wasn't just Jarell walking over.

It was Bree.

At first I was relieved to see her. We could talk about Leila. I could comfort Bree, warn her.

But then she said, "What are you doing here?" Her voice was strained. "Go back to practice, Sky."

I watched him run off, glancing back at me over his shoulder—a little wave of his hand, and my heart collapsed again. Bree was wearing yoga pants and a cropped top that showed off her abs. Why was *she* here? *Because Skylar is her son, Catt. Not yours.*

"I came to see Jarell," I said.

Bree's perfectly plucked brows shot up. "Jarell? For real? You're joking, right? I thought we established that he isn't interested, Catt."

I didn't think this would hurt; I didn't think I cared. I did.

"And shouldn't you be at work?"

"Shouldn't you?" I said.

"I'm off today. I'm teaching yoga to the kids." She cocked her head toward Jarell, Skylar, and the other puppy boys.

"How is Skylar?" I asked. The sun was too hot and I felt faint. My skin itched from the poison sprayed on the grass.

Bree was scowling at me, lines forming on her forehead in spite of the Botox. "Are you fucked-up?"

"No, I—"

"You smell like alcohol. And you look like shit! You're fucked-up, aren't you? You come near my son when you are drunk? You disgust me."

"I'm not drunk," I said.

"You're pathetic. Chasing after Jarell like that? Coming around drunk?"

"Please, Bree."

"No. No fucking way."

"I just wanted to tell you to be careful. Leila—"

"I don't want to talk to you about Leila or anything else. You're fucked-up."

The reality was slamming me now. I might never see Skylar, my reason for living, again after this moment. "You can't do this! He's my son, too." I had said it. I couldn't take it back. "You don't have to see me but you can't take him away from me." Tears were streaking the makeup on my face.

"Your son? How dare you say that? You're always trying to insinuate yourself into this role as what? His second mom? Trying to make him love you more. The other night he called me Bree."

I didn't understand.

She shook her head, lavender locks falling furiously around her face. "He called you Auntie in the same sentence. Auntie."

"You're the one who chose to spend time with loser men over him." I said it softly but loud enough for her to hear.

"What the fuck? What do you know about it? About my life. About what it's like to be a single mom."

"I guess I don't," I said, my Achilles' heel on fire.

Had she hated me for my relationship with Skylar all along? Now she had the excuse she needed.

"You have to stay away from us," Bree said. As if I were the danger in her life. How could she think that? I had to tell her to be careful.

She was crying, too.

Jarell stalked over, gleaming in the sun, larger-than-life. "What's happening here? You okay?" This was directed only to Bree.

She wiped her eyes. He didn't seem to mind her tears, though mine and Skylar's had angered him. His voice was low. "We need you, yoga babe."

She nodded and ran back to the boys.

I screamed. A snake had poked its head out from a hole near my foot. I pointed to it so Jarell would know why I had screamed, but the snake head was gone.

"A snake," I said.

Jarell said, "I think you should leave now."

Skylar looked up. Even from that far away I could see his eyes. The color of the grass in the sun.

Those eyes would never meet mine in that life again.

That night I stopped at a different liquor store. I believed the owner of my local place had looked at me darkly the last time, all-knowing from beneath drooping eyelids. Different place, same purchase. I brought Jack home, stripped to my bra and panties, leaving my cutoffs and tank top on the floor, and flung myself at the couch. Tried to listen to music, but hearing Frank Ocean singing about Egypt, strippers, and rich, unloved children reminded me of Bree—she loved that album—so I turned it off. I drank. I fell asleep. I dreamed.

Of Cyan. He had come into the room wearing a white, button shirt with pearl cuff links and black pants. Was rubbing my ass, teasing my thong up between my cheeks. The fabric pulled against my clit, bringing all the nerves alive. He slapped me gently and then pushed the panties aside and slid a thick finger up inside me while his thumb massaged my clit. I flipped over, and in the same moment he had pulled off my panties entirely. He pushed one of my hands down against his cock, which was huge, bigger than Jarell's, I remember thinking. It strained and peaked the fabric of his black trousers, which were made of a very soft, expensive-seeming fabric. Gabardine. I noticed that his feet were bare and covered in dirt as if he had come through a wet garden. Which made me think of flowers—Stargazer lilies, in particular. I felt overexposed—pink satin and dark fur pelt—and I wished I had gotten a wax. "Take off your bra and show me those nice, big titties," he said. I was surprised because Cyan didn't speak like that. Nor did my brother-in-law (ex?) come into my room and pull off my panties, but somehow my mind seemed to accept that, yet not the other, maybe because the words belonged to someone else, but I couldn't recall to whom. I tugged my breasts out of the cups of my bra, leaving it on; the hooks were digging into my back, making small welts. Cyan took his cock out and began sliding his fingers up and down the shaft while he watched me. With the logic of a dream he told me he had a tiny camera on the end of his penis and that he could take pictures of me from the inside. He was excited to see what he would find.

I woke lying on my stomach, humping the cushions, my fingers searching among them as if I were looking for something in my sleep.

I managed to make it to work that day, fortified with some dry toast and one small shot of whiskey in my coffee, and even did a decent job on five back-to-back clients, although I did burn my hand on the flatiron once. No one seemed to notice my generally fucked-up state, although I imagined (maybe?) Karli frowning at me in the mirror. But when a new client wanted her hair dyed like a pastel rainbow (she'd seen it on a girl who used to work here a while back), it all hit me again. The longing I felt for Bree and Skylar.

Hitting, as in literally. I was pummeled by invisible fists and my skin throbbed with imaginary contusions.

I did not go a-stalking again that night. I could not call my sponsor, who, I believed, had betrayed me and who would not forgive my trespasses. (Shana had called me every day for a week and then given up; I had not called her back once.) The person whose face I could not get out of my mind after the dream I'd had the night before was Cyan, of course. So much had happened since I'd last seen him, and I'd been afraid to reach out before. But when I texted a tentative hello, he did not respond. Swigging some more drink, I called

Dash. As the phone rang, I prayed. Surprisingly, Dash answered, as if my prayer had worked. I wondered what others might be answered. I tried not to ask for sudden, brutal death to obliterate the pain.

"Catt? Are you okay? I heard about the girl from the gym," he said kindly—his voice a gentle scratch—before I had even spoken. "I've been meaning to call you."

The warmth radiating through the phone made me burst into tears. I couldn't speak.

"Catt?"

"Can I see you?" I managed. "Please. I need help."

"Have you been to meetings?" He had pulled away again. "Did you call Shana?"

I continued to cry and beg. Through my tears I heard Dash ask why I sounded like that. "You're not drinking, are you? Catt?" I sobbed at him. He said, "I can't see you. I'm sorry. I have other people to think of now. It's not just me. You need to get to a meeting. Do you hear me? Call Shana right now."

"You can't even give me this?" I yelped. It felt like someone was hitting me with a switch. "What is wrong with you?"

He was quiet for too long a time. Then he said, "A lot is wrong with me. Okay, Catt? A lot. And I am trying to do something about that, and part of it is starting a new life and taking care of my new family."

"What do you even know about family?"

"Not much. I'm trying to learn. You have no idea what I went through growing up."

"You're right," I said. "I have no idea. Because you never told me. You never talked about it. I feel like I know your brother better than I know you."

"What? Cyan? What are you talking about?"

"He came to check on me. We've been talking."

There was silence on the other end of the line.

"What?" I said. That dangerous word.

"I just don't think you should hang out with Cyan, okay?"

"I'm not *hanging out* with Cyan."

His voice was a growl. "Whatever you're doing."

"Why not? Why should you care if your brother is concerned about me or not? You left me. You left!"

I heard a strange sound on the other end and realized that Dash—huge, tatted, punk-rock Dash—was crying softly.

In that moment I loved him, maybe for the first time. Because he was not the mean boy who could protect me, the hot guy who would validate me, or the father of the baby I thought I would die without. He was, like all of the other men I'd slept with, really, a man in pain. Dash had been in much more pain than I realized.

"I can't be around any more fucked-up women. I survived my mother, and instead of running, I kept going back for more. It wasn't your fault, but I'm done, Catt. I can't do this. I'm sorry. I really am sorry. You need to call Shana, not Cyan. You need to get to a meeting. Okay?" He was almost pleading.

So I was like his mother? The person he couldn't

even mention? I'd never even seen a picture of her. She was a monster in his eyes and so was I. *I kept going back for more.* He meant me.

He had hung up.

To torture myself I dragged my bones over to the shelf where I kept our wedding album. Bree had made it for me. It was covered in pink silk printed with black skeletons in wedding veils and top hats, and the pictures were mounted on handmade black paper pressed with pink rose petals. We had thought the album cute and punk rock, not premonitory. Could I find within the pages signs that I had missed? Signs that Dash had chosen me because I was another fucked-up woman? That he would eventually leave me? Dash had no family at the wedding except for Cyan. I had no family at all. It was part of what made our relationship special, I had thought. We were orphans creating our own new clan, which included Bree and Skylar. But what did it mean that Dash's parents and my parents had damaged us to the point that as teenagers we were already trying to drink ourselves to death?

Not even a single picture of Dash's parents existed. He had erased them, and now he would erase me.

In some of our wedding pictures he wore his sunglasses, but in the ones where you could see his eyes there was something flat about his gaze. I was always looking up at him, almost worshipfully.

At two I had fallen in love with a dimple-faced, four-year-old boy named Jakey Zimelman. There was one photo—lost during my early drinking days—of me gazing at him with mad love while he beamed for the camera. Nothing had changed, except that my taste in men had gotten worse; at least Jakey's eyes were warm, even if they weren't looking at me.

I turned to a picture of Bree. She was dancing, but her partner (probably me, while too-cool Baby Daddy watched her from the sidelines) wasn't in the shot. She wore a strapless, pink tulle dress reminiscent of our fake wedding. Her platinum-blond hair was up and her neck looked long, slim, and somehow—due to the angle of the shot perhaps—very vulnerable. The lighting and the reflection from her hair made her face look even smoother and more luminous than it actually was, almost masklike. Her eyes were closed and her lashes cast shadows. I shivered, and a sick feeling crept up my spine like a monkey climbing a tree. There was that resemblance to Leila. But there was something more.

I put down the album and googled Cyan's website. The girls with their doe eyes and legs, their full breasts and streaming hair surveyed me wanly. Leila or Bree would fit right in among them. I took another drink and googled Darcy London. She had started two new clothing lines to go with Mommy's Lil' Punk: Hip Hop Tots and Baby Bling. There was a picture that showed her and Dash wearing matching Ray • Ban Wayfarers, wifebeaters, and torn jeans, running from the paparazzi. Dash was holding her elbow, steering her away, snarling back over his shoulder at the cameras, his extended middle finger blurred out. The baby, Python, bobbed in a pouch on Darcy's chest. He was wearing a black leather visor with silver, star-shaped studs, and one silver earring.

I felt like I was carrying something dead in my womb.

The next evening I got a call from Todd. Or was it Rick? Whichever one it was said they had broken up. I asked if they were okay. Apparently they were still friends, but his voice sounded as if this might not be true. Then he said he was worried about me, and I told him that pinched nerve was acting up again. He invited me over and I said I would think about it, thanks, inwardly cringing at the idea of socializing. He asked if I had heard about Bob.

"No," I said, skin creepily crawling. "What?"

"A detective discovered hidden cameras in the ladies' rooms at Body Farm," Toddrick informed me. "There was lots of footage of Leila, I guess."

I wanted another drink. There was a wildfire inside me. "Do they think he's the . . ."

"They don't know. None of the other girls went to the gym. But they arrested him so there's something going on."

Somehow I felt no sense of relief.

#13

LA summers are a killer. I mean this in the truest sense.

The heat was abominable, but power outages forced us to limit the use of the air-conditioning. And we still couldn't keep our windows open at night with that predator on the loose. My mind replayed scenes of dismemberment again and again as I lay in a small puddle of my own sweat. I dreamed of mountain lions and snakes and wounds that wouldn't stop bleeding. And heads. Decapitated heads. I had heard on the news that an Italian surgeon believed head transplants were a real possibility in the near future.

Someone had been collecting arms, legs, hands, feet, and breasts. What more did they want? Even though Big Bob had been arrested, I didn't feel safe. What if the Hollywood Killer was someone else? Someone even worse?

One night I dreamed of a basement room where I seemed to live. My hair was dyed a deep blue and I had some kind of long forelock falling into my eyes. Women's torsos were suspended from the ceiling, upside down. Blue liquid dripped from the holes where their necks should have been. One of the bodies belonged to Bree. I looked at my hands and saw the blueness staining my fingers. Or perhaps it was just the fluorescent light in the room. I woke with the terror not of the slaughtered but of the slaughterer caught.

In the morning I couldn't stop thinking about Bree. What if she was in danger? What if I could catch the Hollywood Serial Killer? What if I could save her?

That day I traded in my beloved yellow VW Bug for a used gray Honda, and the next morning I waited outside Bree's apartment building. I followed her all the way to her new salon, where I watched her through the window; she was laughing with a magenta-haired woman, reflected in a myriad of mirrors.

A couple of evenings later I drove back to her apartment building and parked out in front. I saw a man sitting in his BMW down the block. As if being controlled by an unseen force, I got up and went over to the car. I rapped on the window with my knuckles. He looked at me.

Stu.

"Hey," I said. "What the hell?"

He jumped, startled. He had been talking on his cell. When he saw it was me, he sneered. "Look who's here," he said, lowering the window and his gaze, down the length of my body, at the same smooth pace.

"Why the fuck are you here?" The adrenaline was forcing the whiskey through my blood faster than normal but not enough to sober me up.

"Why the fuck are you here? I might ask."

"Are you watching Bree? You sick fuck."

Are you watching Bree, you sick fuck? I think he said it, but I'm still not sure.

"I'm going to call the cops," I said. I took out my cell phone.

"You really want to do that with all that booze in your system," Stu calmly replied. His head looked huge. "How many years sobriety do you have again?"

The night of my birthday came back as if I'd fallen down a hole back into the scene. I was looking for Bree in the fun-house maze of my bungalow, wanting her help. She was doing the dishes—too fast, slamming them around, splashing water onto her dress—she wouldn't even look at me. My mouth felt stuffed with dry, sweet cake mix and I couldn't talk.

Back in real time I watched Stu drive away.

I'm still not sure if he was actually there at all.

One night during my "watch," I saw Bree leave her house wearing a short, black cotton dress and motorcycle boots and carrying her camera and Louis Vuitton overnight bag. Skylar was with her but he only had his school backpack. The sun was setting, the sky an odd shade of lilac. I followed them to Baby Daddy's historic seven-story, art deco apartment building in Hollywood, where he and Bree had lived when they first got together, and watched her park and walk Skylar past the cypress trees and in through the glass doors. She didn't stay long.

It is important for me to say, here, that I did not drink that night. I hadn't had a drink since after seeing Stu in front of Bree's apartment building. Not that I considered myself on the way back to recovery; unlike some white-knucklers I was clear that I couldn't do that on my own, long term. But I knew there was something wicked coming, like a storm when you smell metal in the air, and that I would have to face it without the scrim of drink to protect me.

I drove behind her out of the city, along I-10, listening to Savages—music as wailing, dark, and discordant as my state of mind. Night was falling across the brushfire-begging chaparral, and the air smelled of noxious fumes. If aliens had landed, they would think humans were attached to these toxic metal boxes with wheels, that they ate greasy food, gambled, drank beer, worshipped and despised young, beautiful women, and desperately needed hospitals. The aliens would not be wrong. A few scraggly palm trees gave way to dusty shrubbery, and in the distance mountains blackened against a sunset sky. I drove stealthily behind Bree, reciting my Fourth Step inventory in my head to keep from thinking about what I was doing and what she would say if she caught me. I would still list Dash,

Darcy London, Jarell, Carlton, Dean, Stu, Big Bob, the psycho on FU Cupid, Cyan, my mother, my father and Bree, and I would still list the same things that I should have done differently. Shana had moved higher up the list; I'd added Jimmy, peripherally, and Scott was on there for dying, for not getting treatment, for not telling me he was sick. But I was also responsible for everything that had happened.

You know those red stains on the highways? Are those from blood? How do they get rid of those things?

A dead animal lay in the middle of the road, too mangled to identify. I swerved to avoid it and felt my stomach lurch. Once on a trip to the mountains with Dash, I'd seen a deer lying like that, fragilely broken in its darkening blood. It had disturbed me more than it should have, Dash said when I wouldn't stop crying.

"You need to try some meds."

"You know I can't. Of all people you should know."

"SSRIs aren't drugs in the same way, Catt. They just make your body do what it should do naturally. If you'd taken them as a kid, you probably wouldn't have had to start self-medicating."

He was probably right. If I had listened, things might never have gotten to the point they had.

But he would have left you anyway. And so would Bree.

If Bree were an animal, she would be a doe for sure, I thought.

The air hung still and hot; night hadn't cooled it much. We were approaching the real desert, with its vast expanses of empty. The highway wound and I followed Bree at a dangerous distance. She turned onto a dirt road and I had to kill the lights.

Bree, a deer, a female deer, parked and got out of her SUV, adjusted her dress. There was a small building there, middle of nowhere; it looked abandoned except for one lit bulb. The neon sign reading MOTEL was out. Someone had graffitied *Beyond the Pale* across the front wall.

A van was outside. It looked like Cyan's van, but that didn't quite make sense.

I parked behind a small outcropping of rock. Bree didn't seem to notice me; it was as if I had already become a ghost.

For a while I just waited. I saw her enter the building and I listened to the hum of a swamp cooler and the Santa Anas shivering the palm fronds into a whispered frenzy. Time passed; I'm not sure how much. I didn't know what to do. What if she caught me? How would I explain myself?

Finally I got out of my car, the back of my legs suctioning against the vinyl, and snuck around the side of the motel. Weeds brushed my shins and sand gritted my eyes. The air had a faint smell of hot metal.

Through a cracked glass door I saw Bree lying naked, except for her boots, on a bed, her ice-blond hair yanked into a wispy ponytail, her legs spread and her fingers tucked almost shyly between them. Her breasts loomed large, pearled and perfect as the moon that night. Her head was back, her throat exposed. Her eyes looked unfocused. Drugged? There were silver chain bracelets on her neck and wrists. Over her, fully dressed, stood Cyan, taking photos.

What I felt was a strange mix of jealousy, betrayal, desire, anger, confusion, and fear. Why wasn't I there on that bed? Why wasn't someone looking at me that way? Why didn't Bree love me anymore? Was she high? How had I ever believed Cyan desired me? When did Cyan and Bree become close enough to make this happen? And then: Why was Cyan out here in the desert, in this place? Who was he? Besides Dash's brother, the photographer, who was Cyan?

What follows may make no sense. I'm not sure it happened this way, but somehow it all resulted in my current state. And that is what I want to tell, so I will try to recount the events that led up to it as best I can. I was sober, that I know. But I was also, after everything, less than sane.

Cyan pulled something out of his back pocket, and before I really realized what it was (I had only recognized it by the expression in Bree's eyes), I howled Bree's name and threw my cell phone as hard as I could against the glass door. A panel shattered. Cyan whipped around. Bree got up and stumbled screaming through the doorframe and into the desert. Cyan moved toward me holding the thing I'd seen in his hand. A knife. He was evenly tanned; his head was freshly shaven, but not his face—a shadow of stubble defined rather than blurred the angles of his cheeks and chin—and he wore black jeans and a T-shirt and his boots, dusty with desert. The glistering look in his eyes reminded me of a man who has been interrupted just before he is about to come.

"Catt?" he said.

"What the fuck are you doing?" I screamed.

In one motion Cyan grabbed me by the wrists, pinned my arms behind my back, and held me against him with the flat of the knife at my throat. I tried to turn to face him but I couldn't move. For a moment I flashed on how he had stood over me, taking off my clothes. In the desert motel his voice had the same soft tone I had heard in it that night. But how different the words. "She's not going to get far. The drugs will take effect and she'll pass out. Then I'll go get her. Right now, I have things to show you."

"Fucking let go of me. What the fuck are you doing?"

"I'm going to show you something," Cyan said. Beyond the pale motel.

There were many things Cyan made me see that night in the desert. As I screamed and kicked and spat, he tied my arms, stabbed a needle into my leg, and sat me in an old wheelchair. He wheeled me along through empty rooms with broken windows and sand on the floor. Dark rooms. There were tiny squee-ing bats on the ceiling of one dark, dark room. A desert rabbit in a cage. Bones of a coyote and the bones of cats and the bones of birds. The bones of a large dog.

We went into another room. There were chains on the wall. I was already feeling weaker, less able to struggle. Cyan positioned me in front of a black-and-white picture of a woman wearing only a pair of garters and high heels. She was very tall and thin with angular, shadow-casting bones and rapacious eyes. I recognized Cyan's photography. And his facial structure.

"She used to make me take her picture." Cyan sounded like a schoolteacher giving a lesson. "She said I'd be a great artist someday."

I knew who she was, although I had never seen her photograph; Dash didn't want to think about his mother anymore. *I survived one fucked-up woman . . .*

"She left him alone," Cyan went on, as if he knew what I was thinking. "I made sure of that. But kids know what's happening. Look at her." He shook his head. I couldn't read his expression in the dark. "She taught me how to do these," he said.

And then he showed me a series of black-and-white photographs of women.

Strangely—or maybe not—they all looked as if they had already left their bodies. At least the souls had escaped, knowing there was no hope for the bodies. The bodies that were naked, except for their shoes, and bound. Their disembodied beauty was a blank and terrible thing.

I recognized Mandy Merrill and Adrienne Banks

from their smiling pictures in the paper and on TV. Except, in the images I'd seen, they looked fresh and alive. In these made-up, dead-eyed photographs Mandy wore black stiletto boots and a silver choker necklace; she had her hair dyed black and cropped close to her head so her eyes looked even larger in their blankness. Adrienne wore satin pumps and pearls and had her hair in curls. The third woman, with a gardenia behind her ear and high-wedge, ankle-strap sandals, was Michelle Babcock. The fourth young woman was Leila.

Leila's picture made her look like a tan, 1970s pinup with feathered hair. She was wearing one other item besides her metallic platforms. It was the necklace that said *California*. Just like the one I'd found. For a moment I thought, *Did I kill her? Did I kill Leila?* And I wanted to weep but I could not.

All these young women had felt, or would have felt, like threats to me; I would not have invited them over for dinner if, like Michelle Babcock, they were my neighbors, running by in neon shorts. I might not even have learned their names. I would have avoided them, afraid Dash, or, later, if I'm honest, maybe even Cyan, might have chosen them over me.

Cyan had chosen them over me.

The last thing Cyan showed me was the industrial-size refrigerator in the motel basement. By then the drugs he had injected into my leg had fully kicked in and I couldn't scream anymore in spite of what I saw. No one was there to hear me anyway. But what I saw should, by all rights, have dragged screams from the realm of the dead.

The refrigerator hummed like Cyan's pulse and the terrible light in his eyes. In the cold, cold box were what appeared to be a pair of arms wrapped in plastic, a pair of legs similarly wrapped, a pair of hips severed cleanly below the waist and at the upper thigh, and a torso with a pair of once-perfect breasts. I remembered seeing, as a teenager, a picture of a human head stored like meat.

By the refrigerator's greenish-white fluorescence, I saw Mandy reach out to me, though she had no arms. I saw Adrienne balanced on the stumps of her legs, holding Michelle like a baby. What was left of Leila tried to smile at me. I remembered the first time I had seen her smile, the guilelessness, the freckles. She had been a little girl not that long ago. They all had.

My frozen heart cracked into shards. I turned and vomited on the floor, but I did not try to escape. It was the drugs and the knife and the fact that I was tied. But there was something else: maybe somehow I believed that if I gave myself to Cyan, my body and my soul, he would let Bree go.

"I just want her to be safe," I whispered. It took every effort to speak. My face was wet. I was crying but I hadn't noticed it happening. "She has a son."

"She was going to be the face," Cyan said. His voice was a sheet of clear plastic, wrapping my body, suffocating me. He didn't seem to notice that I had thrown up. "She was beautiful. But you have a beautiful heart,

Catt. I need your heart more than I need your friend's
pretty head."

"Please don't hurt Bree, Cyan," I managed.

"This proves it."

Proves? What did he mean?

"You have a perfect heart."

No, I didn't. Not at all.

"You are what I needed to make her," said Cyan.

I knew what he meant before he said it.

"Her," Cyan said.

Perfection.

Cyan told me many things that night. And I listened
because I wanted to know, I wanted to try to understand what had happened. He told me how his alcoholic, heroin-addict mother had made him photograph
her naked and how he did it in order to get her to leave
Dash alone. Although Cyan didn't say what he meant
by this, I could guess. He said he began to enjoy taking
pictures because it was the only time he felt in control
around his mother. He told me how, when his beloved
dog died, he began killing strays and collecting and
photographing their body parts. How he became a suc-
cessful photographer and grew to despise the "narcis-
sists" he worked with. He took home runaways and
prostitutes, promising them modeling careers. No one
ever found out what he did; he became more bold. On
a trip to LA (he hadn't contacted Dash that time; we
didn't know Cyan was there) he had met an aspiring
model named Mandy Merrill, suggested she cut off her

hair, which she did, and photographed her at the abandoned motel he had purchased for shoots. And killed her. Then he met Adrienne Banks and killed her, too. And my neighbor, the one I hadn't let myself get to know—Michelle Babcock. He'd seen her jogging in my neighborhood; she'd smiled and said hello. The night I'd heard the sound outside, he'd watched her from her bedroom window and then slipped back in before I came downstairs and found him. Later he had followed her, given her his business card, photographed her. Killed her.

But Cyan wasn't done.

He'd photographed Leila the day before he stayed overnight at my place. She'd left her necklace behind and he'd put it in his pocket. It had fallen out. Later, he'd bought another one and asked her to meet him again to retrieve it and take a few more shots.

When Cyan saw Leila's necklace on my blog, *Love Monster*, which, he said, he'd followed obsessively since I'd first told him about it, he realized that he'd left the jewelry at my house and worried that I might know something, that it might incriminate him. So he'd come back on the night of my birthday to see if he could get the necklace back. Which he did. He'd brought the cookies in case he needed them, in case he needed to get me high. He'd taken the rest of the cookies with him when he left so no one would find any evidence of what he had done.

The last victim Cyan had chosen was Bree. The woman he was making was almost complete. She would be his revenge upon his mother and the women who reminded him of her. The creature Cyan was making would be his masterpiece, his work of perfect art. She would be his ultimate possession.

"Why Bree?" I asked. My voice felt too thick to fit through my mouth. Why any of them, but especially why Bree?

"She's just as vain, but smarter than the others. Older. Somewhat of an artist. And you love her. But she mistreated you."

I asked with my eyes, *How did you know?*

"She contacted me on my Web site and said she wanted to do a photo session. But really I think it was also her way to get back at you somehow. To come here and see me after she abandoned you like that. She told me what happened after the party."

My mind was trying to put the pieces together but they kept shattering into smaller fragments.

"I never wanted to hurt you, Catt," he went on. His voice had been calm, almost meditative, the whole time he spoke; now it vibrated in his throat. "You are different from them."

I found myself, sickly, wondering if he meant that I wasn't as desirable. Still, even in these last hours when nothing but the sacredness of life, in any kind of body at all, should have mattered, I thought of this. If Cyan had known, he might have killed me long ago. I was just as shallow and vain as any of them, maybe much worse. I told him this. He shook his head. No.

"What about Bree?" I said. "You won't hurt her. She's a mother. She needs to be with Skylar."

I could see him in my mind. As a newborn lying on Bree's white sheepskin coat under the trees, gazing up with eyes like leaves. As a crawling baby with rings of fat around his legs, his chubby-cheeked, gummy grin revealing the delight of motion. Later, missing two front teeth, my charming rogue. At ten, asking me why I couldn't stop smiling at him; it was because his ears, which he hadn't quite grown into, were being folded forward by his baseball cap.

Catt?

Yes, Sky?

The next person you go out with?

Yes?

Has to treat you really, really well.

He had meant Scott, of course.

"Please, Cyan."

"I'll have to go out there and get her soon." He sighed, squinting out through the broken glass door into the vast black. "She'll have fallen."

"She didn't see anything. She doesn't know you did all this."

"She was never really your friend."

I tried to shake my head no, but it felt too heavy. *She was scared, that's all. You're wrong.*

Later, there would be sirens, but I could not yet hear them. If I had, would I have fought harder against Cyan, spurred on by hope? Or would I have given in anyway, sacrificed myself? A part of me believed that if I gave of myself, gave all I had, Bree and Skylar would be safe.

Cyan took a few steps away from me and smoothed his hands over his scalp, examined his tapering fingers. "I need you," he said.

Then, before the sirens came and the police officers arrived, Cyan took my heart. From my body. A body that had always been perfect because it had been alive.

I think of my nine deaths, my nine lives. There had been my life up until Dash left me and Darcy London had his baby. There had been Jarell and Dean and even Carlton, whom I might have loved in spite of his harmless fetishes and his potentially harmful wife. There had been the loss of Cyan before I realized who he really was. Scott's death had been the most brutal loss of them all. I had died at my thirty-seventh birthday party, severed, ultimately, from Bree and, worse, from Skylar.

Now there are no more lives left. All that I have is this—my love for the living, and for the dead.

Love is not the monster, not at all. True love is the thing that makes life bearable. That reveals life's beauty. Love is the monster's opposite.

I will watch over the ones I love, I tell myself—in this undefined vortex of time, in this place between life and death, while I still have a will, while I can still think thoughts and create this final inventory of sorts—as I cross over and turn into particles of light above the Pale Motel. As I spin in the vastness of the universe where bodies matter not at all. I turn and turn and turn and fall, into union with the ones now gone, with the love I never recognized before. . . .

Acknowledgments

I would like to thank the following people for their help: Karen Clark, Laurie Liss, Brandie Coonis, Denise Hamilton, Jessa Marie Mendez, Christopher Bird, Jeni McKenna, Michael Homler, Lauren Jablonski, Jessica Preeg, Jessica Hatch, Joan Higgins, Charlie Blakemore, and Jeffrey Hirsch.